Directions
for an
Opened Body

STORIES

Kenneth J. Harvey

The Mercury Press
(an imprint of Aya Press)
Stratford, Ontario

The publisher gratefully acknowledges
the financial assistance of the Canada Council
and the Ontario Arts Council.

Forthright and pre-eminent appreciation must be extended to my
editor, Beverley Daurio. Without her singular trust and vision, this
book would not have been produced.
Thanks must also be offered to the Explorations Program of
the Canada Council, for providing funds which aided in
the completion of this project.

Some of the stories in this collection have appeared or are
forthcoming in the following publications: *Atlantic Advocate,
London Magazine, Matrix, Scrivener,*
and *Sunk Island Review.*

Production co-ordination: The Blue Pencil
Typeset in Times and printed and bound in an edition of 1000 copies
at Coach House Press, Toronto.

Sales Representation: The Literary Press Group.
The Mercury Press is distributed in Canada by
University of Toronto Press, and in the United States by
Inland Book Company (selected titles) and Bookslinger.

THE MERCURY PRESS
(an imprint of Aya Press)
Box 446
Stratford, Ontario
Canada N5A 6T3

Canadian Cataloguing in Publication Data

Harvey, Kenneth J.
Directions for an opened body

ISBN 0-920544-77-0

PS8565.A678D57 1990   C813'.54   C90-094191-X
PR9199.3.H378D57 1990

Directions
for an
Opened Body

Craving comfort from each other
we sight directions for the closing
of our opened bodies.

For

Joanne Lee Harvey

1959-1980

CONTENTS

Open House

One

MARGO DOESN'T like the way I'm spilling tea bun crumbs on the living room carpet, so I kick over the stereo and scream, "I'll drop crumbs on my own fucking carpet if I choose to."

The pressboard coffee table snaps in half when I jump up and stomp it with both feet. I almost lose my balance, stumble back on one leg. This only makes matters worse. My temper really lets loose and the couch goes over next. I push it with both hands, then wheel away and swipe the fake brass clock from the mantlepiece. It lands upside down and something clicks; the ticking suddenly loud and defined. The love seat tumbles easily. I kick it four or five times, then hurl the cushions against the bookshelves. Margo's books drop like ducks in a shooting gallery. The television sits there like something stupid: blank, uncaring face. I'm still wearing my steel toe boots from work, so I bend back my leg and lean into it.

The explosion makes Margo shriek.

"You're god-damn crazy," she screams from the hallway. I hear the rattle of her keys as she pulls on her down-filled jacket.

"I've had enough of this pestering," I shout. My head is crammed with years and years of the same sound; Margo's voice, whining. The torment needs to bust out. I want to keep

9

shouting but then the door slams, so I race for it. I grab two of her coats from the wall rack, yank open the door and throw them out into the snow.

The cool air rushes into my lungs. It slips through my clothes, chilling the sweat on my arms and legs.

Margo is backing out in her Chevette. She cuts the wheels too sharp and hits the sidewalk, then nails the real estate sign that's set up there. It's one of those wooden signs like a sandwich board that they use for open houses.

"I'll sell the house myself," I shout after her car. "You watch me." I slam the door, spin around and punch a hole in the gyprock. Then I grab the bannister and take the stairs two at a time. The bedroom door is open when I get there and everything's neat as a pin.

I'VE GOT THE SMASHED frame of our wedding photo in my hand when I swing open the front door.

Our real estate agent smiles at me, but then thinks twice about it when he sees the look on my face. His name is Keith and he's the one who found this house for us. We got a deal on it. A real bargain. The dream house of a lifetime.

"Hi," he says. "First customers. You ready?" He leans a little to his left and glances down the hallway.

I nod, "Oh-yeah."

Keith lifts his hand and turns to introduce the couple behind him. "This is Mr. and Mrs. Harper."

"Okay," I say to them. "All right." I spin around and stomp toward the kitchen. "Come in," I shout. "Come on." Halfway down the hallway, I stop and look back over my shoulder. I wave my arm. "Come in, come in. I'm just fixing the refrigerator."

Two steps take me up into the kitchen. The refrigerator is on its side and the door is open and flat to the floor. The tiny bulb is on in there and the food looks pretty strange all to one side like that.

"Look at this," I say to Keith when he steps up. The Harpers stay behind him. They wait and quietly lean in, assessing the damage; smashed dishes everywhere and cupboard doors torn clean off. The kitchen table is upside down in the corner like a stiff moose. The Harpers stare at the socks I've put on the metal legs. They look baffled.

I hold up the smashed frame of our wedding photo.

"What do you think of that?" I ask them.

Mrs. Harper shakes her small head. Her hair is light and wavy and her jaw is a little wide. She squints and her thin lips tighten.

Keith looks at the refrigerator.

"You have a break in?" he asks, quietly, with a sense of dread.

"Yeah, the worst break in I ever saw." I slam the frame down onto the counter. Bits of glass pop up, then settle, and I grab Keith's arm. "Come here. I need a hand with the stove. It's on the fritz. I don't know. Here, edge it out of the corner. Grab it there. That's right. One, two, three. Up. Got it? All right, out. That's it. Almost, almost. Okay. Now, down. Watch out. Step back. I got to check the bottom. The trouble's down there."

Keith steps back and looks at the Harpers. He raises his hand to them as if to say, This won't take long. The Harpers are watching me with interest as if I'm the repair man they've been waiting for their entire lives.

I shove the stove onto its back. It drops with a lot of noise and everyone flinches back at least two steps. I bend over and open the oven door. I let it go and listen to the force of it slamming, the steel racks rattling inside.

"Don't you think that's funny," I tell them. "Gravity's a funny thing when you let it have its way. Huh?"

Keith nods. He looks back at the Harpers. Mrs. Harper smiles politely. Mr. Harper doesn't do anything. He just stands there, biting his pale lips. Then he glances at his watch without reading the time. A second later, he glances at it again.

"MY WIFE LIKES to keep things tidy," I tell them. "This is the den. It was a bedroom, but now it's a den. Maybe it could be a baby's room. My wife reads in here. Quiet type. Likes to

11

read." I smile at them, then sneer at the shelves – the rows and rows of books along the walls. I shake my head. "Look at all these books. All just paper. Can you figure that?"

"Where is Margo, anyway?' Keith asks. "Is she here?"

"Out shopping. She's gone shopping. For new stuff. You can imagine, right? Come on, follow me."

I turn out into the upstairs hallway and lead them into the bedroom. The big one. Our bedroom. The mattress is off the box spring, but the dresser is in its proper place, only upside down.

"My God!" gasps Mrs. Harper.

"Try opening those drawers," I say to them. "It's useless. Never do it. I tried. It's gravity again, like I said. Gravity."

"Did you call the police?" asks Mr. Harper, coughing to clear his throat.

"What?"

"The police?" He holds out a hand like he's trying to be sincere. Like he's saying, Friend, I know what you're feeling.

"Yes, yes, of course," I say, staring at his hand. "They were here."

"And what did they say?' asks Keith.

"Say?" I shake my head. "Forget that." I turn my attention to Mrs. Harper. She's wearing a nice yellow dress with white flowers down the front. She can't be more than thirty. She's wearing flesh-tone nylons and blue dress shoes.

"Nice dress," I say. Then I think, It's a summer dress and here it is – winter. This bothers me for a second but not as much as it'd bother Margo if she was here.

"Thank you." Mrs. Harper forces a smile.

"You're about the same size as my wife." I check her out and she knows what I'm doing. She looks away, out the window. Her hips are a little narrower than my wife's and she's smaller around the chest.

Mr. Harper coughs.

"You have to excuse the mess," I say to him.

"Don't worry," says Mrs. Harper, looking back at me and shyly smiling. "It must have been a terrible shock."

"That's not all," I say. "Follow me. You won't believe this."

"I SAVED THIS for last." I sit on the back of the overturned couch. "What's fun for some."

"Vandals," says Mr. Harper shaking his head at the smashed television. He frowns and slowly takes in the room. The sleeves of his raglan are a couple of inches too long for his arms, and he looks stupid. He nudges a plant holder with the tip of his shoe. The ceramic pot is empty. The plant is elsewhere.

"Up there," I say, pointing like I just spotted something flying overhead. "There's the plant." It's up on one of the long blades of the ceiling fan. "What a shot!"

Mrs. Harper stands in the center of the room with her mouth open and her arms dangling by her sides as if the house is hers. Occasionally, a soft gasp escapes from her lungs when she sights something delicate that's come apart.

"This is amazing," says Mr. Harper. He lifts a pack of cigarettes from the pocket of his overcoat. "Why would anyone do something like this?"

"It's just horrible," says Mrs. Harper. She's going to cry any minute. No question. Her lips are trembling and she keeps moving her fingers like they're stiffening up on her.

"Mind if I smoke?" asks Mr. Harper.

I stand and move in front of him, bend and push the on / off button on the television. Nothing happens. I smile up at him. "Nothing," I say. "Not a blink." Standing, I pull a pack of matches from my jeans pocket and flick one to life right in front of his face.

"Thanks," he says, tipping back a little.

"No problem." I wait for him to get the thing going, then I toss the lit match onto the carpet.

Keith pops out from nowhere, drops to his hands and knees and quickly blows out the flame.

I shake my head and whack my forehead with the butt of my hand. "I don't know what I'm doing," I tell them.

"THERE'S SOMETHING ELSE you haven't seen."

"What's that?" asks Mr. Harper. Smoke streams from his

13

mouth. In an attempt at nonchalance, he tries to blow "O"s, but nothing comes of it. He licks his lips like bits of tobacco are stuck there, only his cigarette's got a filter. His eyes are nervous when they meet mine.

Mrs. Harper stares too. She joins her hands in front of herself and stays silent. Then she whispers, "Something else?"

"The veranda. It's off the bedroom. There's a door. You remember the other door? I forgot to show you the back yard. One of the better points of the house. The veranda. For suntanning. Summer, I mean. You know, topless." I smile and pinch my nose to hold back a laugh.

They follow me up the stairs, more out of interest in the wreckage than in the house, as if it's a tour; some kind of cave or ruin and I'm the guide. I'm the one who knows everything about this. I've studied up over the years. I can point out every invisible pile of bullshit so they don't get their shoes dirty. I can show them the places where the action went down. I'm an expert.

"Look." I pull open the door to the veranda and Keith leads Mr. Harper out there. I hear Keith explaining about the back yard and the new fence and the shed. Perfect for lawnmowers and garden tools and hiding old dead girlfriends. They both laugh.

Mrs. Harper waits at the doorway. She doesn't move an inch. Watching her from behind, I wonder if she's even breathing. Her hands are joined behind her back and she's staring at the side of the house next door.

"You're about the same size as my wife," I tell her. She turns her head and looks at me. I move for the closet and fold open the door. Reaching in, I start throwing out blouses, skirts and dresses.

"Here," I say. "These come with the house."

The rail's suddenly bare, but I want to toss more, like I'm throwing stuff out from inside of me. I turn and see that Mrs. Harper's standing close to the wrecked bed and she's crying.

"I'm sorry," she says with a hand to her mouth. "It must be terrible."

"Everything comes with the house. The pictures. All the

14

clothes." My eyes search the room. "Even those. The photo albums." I rush over and grab the three binders from the shelf by the window. "Here." I push them into Mrs. Harper's hands. "Take them."

"I can't," she says, softly. But she gently takes them all the same.

I nod again, "Go ahead. Have a look. Take a peek. You understand what's in there?"

"Pictures," she says. Her eyes are wet and blurred by tears.

"They're like a consolation prize," I tell her. "When there's nothing left, you get these."

She holds them out to me, but I won't touch them.

"No," I tell her. "You keep them."

Mrs. Harper holds the binders. Her chest shudders with sobs and I know she understands what really happened. Maybe she's seen it before. Maybe she's felt it in the flesh. She's shivering like she has. I think of taking hold of her, moving her to the bed and lying there with her – still and silent – just for comfort. She stands stiff, trembling, trying to hold onto herself. She watches me as tears flood from her eyes.

I step forward and grip her arms. The binders pry into my stomach, then drop to the carpet. I lean closer and kiss her sweetly and delicately, and even sweeter and closer when she presses her lips forcefully to mine and opens her mouth for me.

Two

"CALL ME," I say, waving from the doorway. I lean back into the house and throw out two handfuls of Margo's shoes.

Mrs. Harper looks at the coats and the footwear stuck in the snow on the flat front lawn. She seems more scared now than anything.

"You prick," shouts Mr. Harper, grabbing his wife's arm and guiding her toward the car. He puts her in her seat and shuts the door, then climbs into the Subaru. His door thuds closed and the engine turns over and idles as smoothly as Mr. Harper could ever want it to.

Mrs. Harper stares at me, while Keith leans in Mr. Harper's

window apologizing and giving him the run-down on other properties. But Mr. Harper isn't interested. He rolls up his window on Keith as Mrs. Harper rolls down hers and stares. She just keeps staring until the car glides away. Further on, she even turns her neck to get one final look.

Keith strolls back toward my driveway. He's watching the ground and chewing on the insides of his mouth. I step out into the snow. I bend down and scoop up two handfuls of the white stuff and start patting it together into a snowball. My blue and white flannel shirt is open to the waist and the chill is refreshing against my chest.

Keith won't look at me. He opens his car door, but just stands there as if he's going to say something. Then he shakes his head and turns back to the sidewalk for the sign. Folding it up, he lifts it under his arm and carries it with both hands back to his car. When he gets there, he leans the sign against his bumper. He slips in a key and pops the hatch.

I step out further onto the lawn until I'm knee-deep in snow. My boots are solid and insulated so this doesn't bother me. My hands work quickly, shaping the snow into a hard, white ball. The kind that every kid dreams of making.

Keith lifts the hatchback, slides the sign in, then shuts the hatch with serious force. Walking around the side of his car, he won't look at me or the house, as if we're not here at all. I know what he's saying to himself. He's saying, No more open house, no more open house, as he climbs in and starts the engine. His windshield wipers come on even though it's not snowing. Then he turns them off. I can see his face behind the windshield. He's looking over at the house next door. I look there too, and see an old guy stepping out onto his concrete walk with a chihuahua on a leash. I've seen the guy a million times, but I couldn't come up with his name if my life depended on it.

"How's it going?" he says, straightening his wool cap on his head. The cap's got a big round tassle on its peaked tip. It's green and he's got on big green mittens too.

"Not too bad," I say.

Keith watches the old guy for a while, or maybe he's just in a daze, then he pulls out of the driveway. He swerves back in a neat arc and straightens before pulling away fast. I see someone's drawn dollar signs in the frost on his rear window.

"Taking the dog for a walk?"

"You bet."

"Nice day for it," I say, patting the snowball with my bare hands. I squeeze the surface until it feels smooth and solid as cold steel. My feet are still warm, even though my breath is puffing in the air. My fingers are a little frozen. They don't feel the rough grains of the snowball. Numb and thick like this, they just sense the smoothness.

"Nice air," I say, taking a deep breath.

"Perfect." says the man, strolling by my front lawn.

"Who's home at your place?" I ask.

"No one," he says, stopping and watching me. The tiny dog sits on the sidewalk and stares up the street.

"You need something?" asks the old guy.

"No. I'm selling my house," I say, tossing a thumb back toward my open door. "Open house today."

"I saw the sign," he says, but he doesn't seem to notice that the sign is gone. He raises his hand; the one that's holding the leash, and points. "Those your clothes?"

I look behind me. Then I look at him and frown, shaking my head.

"No way," I tell him. "Uh-uh. Someone else's."

"My wife left me once too," he says. He stands there and looks down at the dog like the tiny mutt holds the key to all of this. The dog stares up at him. "That was a long time ago," he says to the dog. The dog yaps and the old guy nods, "Isn't that right, my vicious little baby. You're my only girl now." The dog yaps again and the old guy peers up at me and laughs.

"She's a smart dog," he says.

"I don't doubt it one bit. A lot smarter than some people I know."

"You bet," says the old guy, turning his head toward a shiny black car that's coasting up the street. The driver must be counting house numbers. The car slows, rolls ahead a little, pauses. I can't see who's in there because of the glare against

17

the dark tinted glass. The car's either a Lincoln Continental or a Cadillac. I can't tell them apart anymore. The only thing I know is that the boys in Detroit are making both of them too short for my liking. The car stops in front of my house, then pulls into the driveway.

The window hums down and I see there's a woman at the wheel. She lets the window go down all the way until it's plain that she's alone in there with an interior full of plushness.

"Is this the open house?" she asks.

"That's right," I say.

"See you later," says the old guy, starting to stroll off and giving a little tug on the leash. The chihuahua isn't paying attention and the collar almost chokes it. The mutt yaps and picks itself up quick. It scampers fearlessly alongside the old guy like it's a doberman who slipped into the wrong body by mistake.

"Yeah," I say. "See ya."

"This is a pretty quiet neighbourhood," says the woman, stepping out of the car and slamming the solid door. She stands in the driveway and studies Margo's clothes sprawled across the lawn. She slowly steps forward, until she's on the slippery concrete walk. It needs shovelling in a bad way, but the woman doesn't seem to mind. She's smiling like there's not a worry in the world, like everything's a joke. Her face is smooth and she's got this fresh, energetic glow. She's not wearing a cap and her honey blonde hair hangs straight down the back of her long brown coat. It's got a fur collar made out of mink or something. She's wearing gloves, too. Tight, brown gloves that match the color of her eyes.

I bounce the snowball in my palm and smile at her.

She smiles playfully but with suspicion, and cautiously inches forward toward the door.

"You're here about the house," I say. I bounce the snowball a couple of more times, then dip my arm back and hurl it high into the sky. The ball sails right over the roof of a house across the street, and drops out of sight. Looking back at the woman, I see she's watching where the snowball went, then she's watching me.

"You own the house," she says, smile widening.

I glance back at my opened doorway. The mattress is just inside, leaning against the wall from where I dragged it down the stairs.

"No, that's not the one," I say. "Someone just broke in to that one. Tore the place up pretty bad."

"Really?" she says. "Wow!"

I point to the house next door to mine. The house that the old guy owns. The old guy and the counterfeit doberman.

"That's the one," I say.

"Oh," she says, looking at the old guy's house.

"That your car?" I ask her.

"Yes," she says.

I struggle through the snow, lift my legs one at a time until I'm standing next to the driver's door. I bend close to the window, cup my hands and stare in.

"That's a nice car," I say, lifting my head to take a look at her. "You're a rich lady. You got it made."

She shrugs her shoulders. "I guess," she says, smiling.

"Can I take it for a spin?"

"Ummm. I don't know. Do you have a license?"

"Of course I got a license."

She laughs like it's the thing to do, "Then I suppose it's okay. Sure. Why not?" She shakes her head and laughs again as if she can't believe how crazy and wild she is.

"I'll just be a sec. I've got to pick up some milk at the store. You go on in and look around and when I come back we'll have tea and biscuits. Cookies." I nod. "Okay? That's a good plan, isn't it?"

"Sure." She shrugs and claps her gloved hands together. "Okay." She backs away toward the old guy's concrete walk. He's got it shovelled real clean. You could eat off it if you were trying to prove a point, which is something I sure as hell am not trying to do.

I open the car door and wait.

"The keys are in it," says the woman.

"Okay." I say. "Make yourself at home. Put the kettle on." I lean in and sink into the plush blue velvet. Then I pull the

19

heavy door shut. "Fix yourself a snack," I whisper. "Throw another log on the fire. Put your feet up. Take a load off." I check out the control panel. It looks like an ad from a classy magazine. The light in here through the tinted glass is something else. And the smell is rich and brand new.

The woman waves from the walkway as I flick the ignition over to instant purr. I watch the woman turn and try the old guy's door. It's open and she steps up and in. She waits a second, watching me, before she shuts the screen door, then the inside wooden one.

I turn on the FM stereo. A deejay's voice pours forth – deep and luxurious. His voice was made for this car. No doubt his voice is covered under the warranty. It comes from everywhere at once and is soothing like warm water forming words.

Backing out, the car rolls like mercury. The steering wheel turns with one finger. I touch the brakes and a shiver streams up my spine. The gear shift clicks smoothly and I glide off, wondering where this car will take me.

The old guy is coming up the other side of the street. He's talking to his dog, but the dog isn't listening. Instead, it's watching me as the car cruises by. The dog yaps. It can't see me through the tinted glass, but it knows what it's doing.

I touch the horn and the old guy waves. He stops and sweeps his arm through the air, waving and smiling. The dog keeps yapping up a storm. It lurches forward, snapping at the end of its leash.

I take the corner like I'm leaning into a cloud and glance in the rearview. The old guy's still standing there. He's got both hands cupped around his mouth. And he's shouting.

The dog's busted loose. Its tiny, furious legs scamper after the car as its leash drags through the slushy street. There's no way it'll stop chasing me. It knows who I am. Yapping, *Bastard. Home-wrecker. Thief.*

Orderly

I IRON MY WHITE hospital pants on the living room carpet. They must be creased and crisp like the bedsheets themselves. The white t-shirt is fine as is. I stand, slip on my pants, then pull the t-shirt over my head, smooth it across my broad chest.

At fifteen minutes to eight I leave the house. It will take ten minutes to drive, four minutes to enter the building and change, and precisely one minute for the ride up the elevator.

My shift commences at eight o'clock. It could be a.m. or it could be p.m. Shifts alter but the actions remain the same. What happens happens with definite structure. Within an institution such as this the need for routine is intrinsic.

I instill order. No matter how extreme the tactics, the preservation of order must be foremost and unquestionable.

FOR INSTANCE: Mrs. Gallant is between medication. She asks me to see her husband. Can she call him? Can I lend her a quarter? I comply and guide her to the pay phone in the social room. She dials. The number has been disconnected. She listens to the recorded voice. It repeats itself. She listens three times, then returns the receiver to its cradle.

"Something's wrong," she says, slowly, baffled. "The number's out of order."

"Perhaps it's being repaired," I offer.

21

"Yes," she says, vaguely.

"Let's go back and try later."

"Yes."

We walk together. She is thinking of her husband. Her husband was killed in a blaze only three months ago. A small child was trapped in the house as well. She hears it crying.

When they pulled out the still, smouldering child, she screamed, "He's crying, give him to his mother." The medication fades and she hears it crying. She halts now, bends her head as if listening to a distant voice. Her lips are slightly parted and her meek face begins to tighten.

The nurse sees us coming.

"Mrs. Gallant," she says. "I have something for you."

Mrs. Gallant is startled by the voice. With complete humility, she stares at the nurse and takes the tiny plastic cup of pills. She swallows them, quickly and easily.

"I'll call again later," she says, handing the empty cup to the nurse. The nurse nods.

"Yes," I say.

Mrs. Gallant steps back, across the threshold of her room as if reversing. I close the door and lock it.

I will not see Mrs. Gallant again for the remainder of my shift. In this institution she may believe anything that calms her. The preservation of order means trust in lies. Patients may do as they choose, believe in the outrageous. This is order and it is something I do not deny.

MR. ELLIOT'S face is vicious with intention. He is watching television but he is watching me through the corner of his dark eyes. He wants to say something to me, but instead he scowls at Mrs. Penney.

"Cunt," he barks.

Mrs. Penney tut-tutts. "I know," she says. "Tell someone who doesn't."

"Virgin Cunt Mary."

"Mr. Elliot," I caution. He glances sharply my way.

"Yeah," he says. "Nazi," he says. "Don't tell me who you are, Nazi."

I lift my finger to my lips. "Shhhh."

"Easy," he says, staring at Mrs. Penney, watching her white legs beneath the edge of her cotton skirt.

Across the room, Mrs. Martin is writing words in the air with her index finger. Her lips whisper, along with her actions, reading. She looks down at the book in her lap.

"What're you doing, Mrs. Martin?" I ask, nodding to the pages.

"I'm studying French," she says, grandly flicking back her grey-haired head.

"That's an English book," I say.

"I'm studying French in English," she snaps.

"I understand," I say, and I almost do understand. There lies the key: in that one word – almost.

Returning to the door, I stand and fold my arms. The television is playing an old romance. Black and white. They are kissing on the screen. Mr. Elliot begins undoing his pants and so I move for him and quickly lead him away.

In the corridor, Nurse Dunphy looks up from her station. Her uniform is unbearably white. She smiles sweetly. I ignore her. A job is a job.

"Hello, Mr. Hayter," she says to me.

I am silent.

"Where are you taking Mr. Elliot?"

"To his room."

"He's been naughty again, eh?"

I move up the hallway, my arm around Mr. Elliot's shoulder as if we are old pals. All the while, he stares at me. He stares at the side of my face, his hands down his pants, thrusting violently.

"My room," he says, smiling, smiling victoriously as he scampers into privacy.

I look down the long corridor and Nurse Dunphy is watching me. She waits, taps a pen against the side of her head, then returns to her chart.

Mr. Elliot shouts, "Holy Mary Mother Of God Pray For Us Sinners Now And At The Hour Of Our Death." I open his door and see him drop to his knees with both hands savagely clutching and pumping.

"Amen," he says, gasping for mercy. "Amen, amen ..."

NURSE DUNPHY is blonde with her hair swirled up into a bun and clipped beneath her nurse's hat. She has a young thin face. It is attractive with long lashes and teeth that are a touch crooked. She is good humoured and insists on teasing.

"Get back to work," she says as I pass her station.

"There's only Mrs. Penney," I say.

"She's enough."

In the social room, Mrs. Penney (she is not married, but it is customary to refer to the female patients as Missus) is crying with her head in her hands. I look up at the screen and see the image fading out. "The End" fades in along with booming music and then the tiny, hazy credits roll.

Cry, I say to myself. Cry, cry, cry. It is therapy. I know that much.

Mrs. Penney lifts her eyes to me. They are tiny and pink and she is smiling.

"How's my hair?" she asks.

"Fine," I say, returning the smile.

"Look," she says. She pulls down the collar of her pink sweater. I see the thick scar running down to the top of her breast. I can see no further but I know the scar continues down. She was cut as a teenager. A maniac with a knife and then later the need for heart surgery. The incisions scarred her insides as well, implanting obsession beneath the lifted line of scar tissue. She is engrossed with her appearance.

"Look," she says. Reaching down into her brassiere, she pulls up her left breast. She taps the thick nipple as if sending messages in morse code. She taps it frantically.

"Understand?" she says. "I love you. I love you."

"Time for bed," I say and she nods with the enthusiasm of one about to receive a gift.

"Yes." She follows me without question.

Nurse Dunphy says, "Tuck her in real good." She speaks with her nurse's voice; the one that is set in a compassionate mode. It is up-tempo and soothing. Trouble free. Breezy.

Mrs. Penney takes my hand. Her fingers are small and chubby. They are wet with perspiration, or perhaps fluid of another nature.

"You understand why we'd never get along," she says.

I nod sympathetically.

When we reach her doorway, she leans close, steps up on her tiptoes and kisses me.

"Goodnight," she says.

"Goodnight," I say.

She looks up at the ceiling as if at a brilliant moon. She senses the calm light brushing her face. She sighs.

"It's for the best," she says. I agree and watch her step into the room. Inside, she stands close to the small, square window of her door. She watches as I lock it. She hears the sound and her face suddenly changes.

"Don't look at me," she shouts through the glass. "KILLER." I turn my back before I can hear the threats issue from her. I step away and move toward the social room. It is quiet and I glide across the tile.

The new movie concerns a mental institution. It is very old and the acting is forced; overly dramatic. I laugh at that and sit on the couch. Cross my legs. Fold my arms. Order.

In a moment Nurse Dunphy joins me. She shows me a run in her nylons, how far up it rides.

"Up to here," she says. "Look," she says and I think of Mrs. Penney revealing herself.

Nurse Dunphy lifts her skirt higher until I see she is not wearing underwear beneath the white nylons. She turns around to innocently show me her behind.

"See how the seam runs right up the crack of my ass?" She doesn't wait for a response. "Isn't that the prettiest thing?"

I watch the screen. A nurse's black and white eyes are wide. Her long lashes flutter as she fills a syringe. It is a silent movie.

"We're on all night," says Nurse Dunphy. "Later we'll go visit Mrs. Penney. Have some fun. Three of us."

I nod and she skips merrily from the room as if all is well; all matters reduced to a carefree level of operation.

"Reports, reports," she says on her way to her station.

Someone says to me, "Death is perfect order." I turn and look at the doorway, but no one is standing there. The light from the corridor is clean and reassuring. The social room is dim. The lights are off and I sense the patients stirring in darkness.

It is only the pulse from the screen that gives light. The institution of television is quite appealing. People enter willingly and remain for their entire lives. A schedule set by the television guide. Order in one form or another. Direction. We must lead each other in a calm, uneventful direction. The craving of order. Books set in rows, cars parked side by side, forms in triplicate, perfect human symmetry. Neat, clean lines guiding us straight to death. Symmetry. Cemetery.

Up on the screen, the nurse is chasing a male patient around a table. The patient throws over the table and laughs with his head tossed back, freezes stiff and begins to howl. The nurse moves beside him. She loves the patient. She tenderly swabs his forehead. Then, when he has calmed, she thrusts the hidden needle into his arm. Order. It is a silent movie. I cannot hear the scream. It is silent, or the sound is turned down. One or the other.

"Death is perfect order," says the television nurse, but I know she is not saying it at all.

Orange Shadows and a Sound that is the Two of Us

for Janet

THE SMELL OF CREAM rubbed into sunburnt skin. She moves the straps away with two fingers. I feel the heat. The heat melts the cream. And she makes a noise as if I am rubbing the cream into a place inside of her, a place where only my fingers can touch and are permitted. It is a sound that I alone can draw from her, but only with her. A sound that is the two of us.

"Kiss it," she says, unclasping and removing the swimsuit.

I lower my lips and kiss her flaming skin. I guide her down on her round belly, onto the bed. She is with child and is worried. The sunburn. Will it hurt the child? Her belly sinks and fits into the soft mattress.

"Careful," she says as I lie on top of her. "My shoulders."

"I won't touch them."

"It's okay," she says. "You know it's okay. We can do it for another month."

"I know."

The sounds come from her and from me. The sounds turn to breathing. They are not simple sounds, but are filled with the rich complexity of pleasure. They swirl and entwine like vapourous fingers. If our throats were torn away by some loveless creature of misunderstanding, the sounds would still come, not from our throats but from the movements of our skin like whispers of the same.

"I want to see it on my skin," she says, rolling over. I ease up

27

and out and let her see, but she cannot see because of her belly. She touches me there and feels me wet her. Then her fingers caress the milky fluid into her skin.

"I'm rubbing you into me," she says in a special voice to which she rarely treats me. "It all started with this."

"And with you," I say.

"Yes." She leans up on her elbows and motions for me to kiss her. I lower my lips to hers and the warmth there draws the sound from both of us at once.

I stand from the bed. She rolls over on her round belly again and I watch her. I step to the balcony and open the glass sliding door. There are long orange shadows stretching across the manicured bowling green below, across the empty tennis courts, over across the street they stretch to the beach and the small fishing boats. The scene is calm and drawing warmth. I feel myself inside of her again.

"Are you okay?" I call back into the room, but do not step in. I stay on the balcony and wonder what all of this would mean without her and without the child. What would I do without this child I do not yet know but feel is already so much a part of me?

"The sun is so beautiful here," I say, but she does not reply and I know, by her silence, that she is sleeping and smiling for what is inside of her and for me. She is smiling even for the sunburn for it is a part of everything that draws us together.

I step back inside and carefully slide the door closed. Her face is turned towards me on the pillow. Her eyes are closed and her mouth is open and the strips and patches of white skin are so prominent against the sunburn on her back and down her legs. I see the sunburn begins to white out along her sides where her belly begins to round out.

She is asleep and I lie next to her, holding my breath to my fragile movements so as not to wake her. When I am lying flat, I stare up at the ceiling. I ask myself, Why are things so perfect sometimes and other times so treacherous and dislocated? I turn to her and move my face close until I can feel her breathing. She doesn't wake and I stand again after kissing her on her open lips, stand next to the bed and watch her until she wakes.

"What're you doing?" she asks with another special voice; one of sensuality and waking.

"Watching you," I say.

"Nice," she says and smiles. Her eyes ease shut again as she abandons me for sleep. Like the child that is so perfectly curled and shaped inside of her, she leaves me with a sleeping silence.

I sit in the cushioned chair by the sliding glass door and pull open the heavy drape. Orange shadows slip into the room and slip across her skin. She closes her lips and smiles as if it is me who is touching her. Love, like the sun, holds treachery and beauty; the burning and the orange shadows. For now, I take the orange shadows and forget the burning. What else can I do when I see the orange shadows touch her that way?

I stand and touch her and she wakes and pulls me down with her. Even though she is still half asleep, she wants the touch.

"I love you," she says.

"I love you, too," I say, and I feel her sunburn and the orange shadows at once. "I love you more than anything," I say.

"Me too," she says and presses her round belly close to mine, opening her eyes for me, everything done for me. "All the love I have is right here," she says. "And it's all yours and it's the child's too. But it's one." She blinks, unexpectedly as if she does not understand what she has just said, but understands it completely.

"You take another nap," I say.

"Don't go," she says, holding.

"Okay," I say.

"Close your eyes."

I smile and close my eyes.

"Now, I'll close mine," she says, but when I open my eyes I see she is watching me and we both come close to laughing and kiss and move as close to each other as we can but do not sleep. We watch and touch and feel the luxury of skin rich with orange shadows.

"Again," she says and rolls over onto her belly despite the sunburn, turning her cheek to the pillow so I can watch her face and see what it is I am doing to her. Everything that means

29

anything is there in how her face changes when I move inside of her, drawing forth the sound that is the two of us. The sound that is alive with silence and expectations of conception. The silence of life within two giving life to one.

The Profound Liberation of Roy Purdie

FOR THE MAJORITY of his sixty-four years, Roy Purdie was not concerned with the pressures or vague sensations of objects pressing against his skin. Only because these sensations were not realized did they not concern him, for it could never be said that Roy Purdie was an unconcerned man. He had worn a watch without the slightest notice of its tight, awkward hold on his wrist. He had sported a felt hat to and from work at the dealership. It rested neatly and slightly tipped back on his head and its snug, oval fit paid him no bother. His heavy, lined overcoat – which he wore in summer and winter – was merely something he slipped his arms in and out of. He did not realize the weight of it upon his shoulders, or that it made him slouch.

Realization, however, delivered itself one Tuesday in April when – without warning – Roy Purdie took notice of the wallet in his right pants pocket. Peculiar, he said to himself, shifting in his chair. The wallet pressed slightly into his rump in a way that was suddenly alien. A moment later, he was aware of his sunglasses in the inside pocket of his suit jacket. They were like a tumour, or a giant, brittle bug sleeping in a pouch.

Roy Purdie sat in the cubicle that was his office staring down at his thin wrist. Above him, certificates of sales accomplishments adorned his walls. They were old certificates. If one looked closely, the dates would uncover memories of the purest quality. Next to his desk there was only sufficient room for a single chair to accommodate the client. If the client happened to be a couple, then one of them was forced to stand.

The business was the only Chevrolet dealership in Point Grace; a small city along the eastern seaboard. As with most cities of small population, life was generally uneventful. In fact, Roy Purdie had heard many say that Point Grace was more akin to a small town disguised as a big city.

He wondered why he continued to hear that statement uttered in an unkind tone over the years. If Point Grace was more like a small town, then all the better. All the better for everyone. Who would want to be concerned with the issues of a big city? Life was busy enough, with little time for enjoyment. Imagine the pace of a metropolis.

He nodded slightly to himself as he unclasped the silver strap of his wristwatch and let it drop onto the desk. He stared at its face, watching the second hand smoothly revolve. A strange thought suddenly struck him: Where is that tiny arrow pointing?

Roy Purdie pulled his gaze away from the watch face and examined his wrist. He rubbed the two trails of tough skin that had hardened over the years. The side of the square watch had rubbed against his skin whenever he bent his wrist. The marks were scarlike and he marvelled at their texture. He thought of himself as scarred by his need for a view of time.

Raising and turning his narrow head, he glanced out into the showroom. It was a little past suppertime and the area was still. The cars seemed varnished and dipped in light. Further out, one of the salesmen, Tom Chesley, was moving slowly across the floor. Roy Purdie watched Chesley's shoes. They were brown and dull. Roy Purdie looked up to see Tom Chesley's stern face, but then a second later a smile instantly curved onto Chesley's lips as he saw someone in the distance, approaching.

Standing, Roy Purdie pulled the wallet from his right pants pocket. He tossed it onto his desk and sat again. The sensations were less irritating than they were strangely profound. Roy Purdie noticed the outlines of images. The soft and hard edges.

He seemed to see with a sharper, acute vision. Glancing around his office, he analyzed the faded pictures of older, classic cars. He stared at the new models and experienced a faint pang of disgust at their smooth, bland style. He looked at the corner where the coat tree stood. It was straight and perfectly symmetrical. He imagined lifting his hat and placing it atop his head. He saw himself slipping his arms into the smooth lining of his blue overcoat. He imagined these actions with a vividness that brought him new, unexpected joy.

The seat was hard. He swivelled upon it and opened the deepest drawer of his desk. He lifted out a thick file containing sales contracts for the past month. Flipping through them, his eyes skimmed the names in search of familiarity. The names were like friends to him. He thought back. He considered the personalities of each client. The names strangely connected to faces. After all, he thought, these names were only words. How do they connect to actual images? He wondered, and then he dialed a number just to hear the voice. He dialed, listened and then hung up. His finger probed several other numbers. He listened and saw faces. It was suddenly unnerving.

Roy Purdie stood and stepped back from the file. He turned and swept up his hat from the brass hook. He placed it atop his head and stepped out of his office until he was close to the side of a new car. The lights were bright and he wished for dark sunglasses. He wanted to hide behind dark glasses and simply play with his new, unexplored thoughts. Bending down, he stared at his reflection in the window. He tilted back his hat. He pushed it forward. Then he pulled it from his head and spun it across the showroom as if it was a frisbee. The receptionist at the center booth watched it collide with the wall and land upright on the floor. Then she looked at Roy Purdie. Roy Purdie looked at her and smiled. She returned the smile. They had known each other for years.

"Bored," she called.

"Yes," he said. He thought, Bored. Yes, that's it. No. He shook his head. That's not it. That's too easy. He stepped toward her and showed her the two trails in his skin made from the friction of the watch.

33

"That's something," she said, then motioned to hold on a sec as she answered a line.

"Something," he said to no one in particular. "You're right, that is something." He stared at her. He held up an index finger. "Yes, but what?" he said with wonder.

Roy Purdie moved away from her. He walked back into his office, took off his suit jacket and placed it over the back of his chair. He loosened his tie and popped the top button of his shirt. The change in his right pocket seemed to lean him off balance. He reached in and pulled up the coins in one big handful, tossing the tiny metal circles up into the air. Several coins struck the desktop, while others rolled along the tile. Two red cents wheeled out and shimmied flat onto the showroom floor. He looked down at his shoes. It seemed almost as if he could sense the laces piercing each eye hole. Lifting one foot at a time onto his chair, he tugged free the laces, tied them together, then bounced them off the wall where they dropped onto his desk.

His line lit up with a call. He quickly sat and punched the button. Lifting the receiver, he pressed it against his ear, then held it away. He listened to the distant voice he could barely make out.

"What do you want?" he asked, holding back a laugh. It all seemed so amusing. He hung up.

The elastic of his socks was pressing fiercely into his shins. The hairs beneath the material felt as if they were being gently pulled. The sensation was horrendous and Roy Purdie rolled down his socks to relieve the torment. His skin felt suddenly fresh. He slipped off each shoe and struggled with his socks, pulling vigourously until they recoiled free.

The flooring was cool against his bare soles. He walked out around the showroom, smiling, staring down, savouring the sensation. He crouched down and rolled up the legs of his pants. It was refreshing. He swirled in circles with his arms to his sides.

He stopped suddenly, his head spinning with a joyful imbalance; like magnets of opposite polarities pulling behind his eyes. He staggered over to the receptionist.

"Roy?" she said.

He was smiling, uncontrollably.

"Did you get that call?" she asked with a trace of concern.

He nodded. He said, "I can feel the whiskers pushing through my skin." He scratched the stubble along his jaw.

Her brow creased down the center and she frowned. She lifted a pen, unconsciously flipped it over and tapped it against a message pad.

"Are you okay?' she asked.

He was beaming. He dipped his thin head forward – chin almost touching chest – and smiled like a true romantic. He opened his arms as if for an embrace, then backed away and swirled in huge circles.

"So this is it," he said, over and over.

He unbuttoned his shirt to the waist but left the flaps tucked in. He felt the wind against his skin as he spun. He spun until he collapsed and sat in a giddy clump with the showroom circling him.

"My fingernails grow at a tremendous rate," he said to Tom Chesley who was bent down, helping him to his feet. "If you watch closely you can see them grow."

"I'm sure," said Tom Chesley, discreetly sniffing Roy Purdie's breath for traces of alcohol. Chesley tightly clutched his colleague's arm and guided him up. "Can you stand okay?"

Roy Purdie gently slipped his arm free and backed away. He lifted his hands in front of himself – palms facing up toward the numerous showroom lights – as if to indicate, No sweat. He turned and side-stepped – in the fashion of a vaudeville exit – back toward his office. Once inside, he sat and decided to call his wife. He noticed the hardness of the chair and stood again, hopping on his bare feet and giggling.

Dialing the number, he laughed out loud and shook his head at the obvious humour of it all.

When his wife answered, he said, "What more could you want?"

"Roy?" she said. "Where are you?"

"What more could you want?" he demanded, overjoyed. "More?"

35

"I'm coming home."

"Are you okay? Are you sick?"

"Take off your jewelry, Alice. Take off your shoes. Take off your wristwatch."

"Roy?"

"Take off your socks, your nylons, take out your teeth. I'm taking out mine." He reached into his mouth and pulled down his dentures. He tossed them onto his desk, next to his wallet.

"Roy? What was that noise?"

He stood and stared at everything atop his desk. He smiled and his pink gums sheened, innocently. How could it have all gone this far? he asked himself with exquisite delight. He unhooked his pants, pulled the zipper and let them drop around his ankles. Roy Purdie could sense the hairs on his legs standing on end.

"Roy?" said his wife. "Roy, are you there?"

Ballerina

I PICK AT THE SMALL clumps of thread along the row where my buttons were torn away. My breathing is tight even though I'm lying on the couch staring down at my opened shirt, and stomach. Too many potato chips and chocolates are taking their toll. I've got a sweet tooth that I can't do anything about so there's a need to pop the clip on my trousers to get comfortable, so as not to strangle my stomach.

This shirt is a mess. The right sleeve is torn clean off and the dark hairs on my arm are wet with sweat. My heartbeat is savage; punching in my throat and throbbing at the sides of my forehead. When I close my eyes, I feel like my heartbeat's trying to jolt me off the couch. The trails of scratch marks are stinging along my arms. This thick heat just brings out the sweat.

I want to shout, Maureen. But it won't do any good. She's been here and gone; got her nails into me and tore me up. All I wanted was to know where Amy is. She won't tell me where Amy is. And Maureen's crazy when she doesn't get what she wants. She won't listen to you. I said to her, "Where are you hiding Amy?" and that's when she came at me with her eyes wide, kicking and clawing.

I FLICK THE CHANNELS with the changer and catch a glimpse of everything that's going on. All these shows with children in them make me think of Amy. I turn off the set and push myself up from the couch. I think of taking a look at my face but I know it's scratched up pretty bad so I'll wait till I have a bite to eat before washing the cuts. I can see one of the cuts on the top of my nose. The blood's starting to dry up and it's a rusty-colored line that my eyes keep trying to focus on.

In the kitchen I crack an egg over the frying pan full of brown rice, onion and corn. I stir the works. Something's going to happen soon. My hands are shaking and I can't stop seeing Amy's frightened face and everything is blurring over, so I've got to brace my hands against the smooth edge of the stove and stay like that while the sobs buck in my chest. I know it sounds kind of stupid; a big man like me, but I can't help it. I wipe at my face and my hand comes back with the palm smeared with blood. She must have scratched me bad. But the stinging is nothing compared to how I feel when I think of what Maureen's telling Amy.

AMY'S ONLY FIVE YEARS OLD and good as gold. Her teacher told me that she's one of the smartest, and pleasant as sunshine. She'd answer anything. Always got her hand up in class and she's so small and pretty. Blonde curls. I'm not kidding. And I bought her dresses all the time. I picked them out because Maureen's the working one. I'm out of work since they finished the City Hall Annex seven months ago. So I'd shop for Amy and pick out the prettiest little things you ever saw. Those clothes are so cute I'd stay in the store for way too long looking at everything. The clerk would stare at me like I was some kind of creep. I don't know what people are thinking anymore. The crap on the television has made everyone into something not human at all.

"I got a little girl," I told the woman clerk.

And then the woman smiled as if everything was okay.

"She's the prettiest little thing you could ever imagine," I'd tell all the clerks.

KENNETH J. HARVEY

I got a little girl. You understand what I'm saying. Anyone with children understands what I'm saying. You know what it's like; how tiny and perfect they are in your arms. And the things they say that could make you cry. Then someone takes them away from you and you don't feed them anymore or read to them anymore or put them in bed at night. Nights just empty now and quiet as a haunted house. Someone takes them away from you. Someone you don't even love anymore, a stranger. Someone takes your little girl away from you and hides her somewhere. And this someone starts telling the police that you've been doing terrible things to your little girl. Someone tells your little girl things to tell the police, things that make you sick to your stomach to think about, things that make your knees weak and all your bones hollow with pain.

THE POLICE HAVE been here once and asked to see pictures of Amy. I took the framed photo from over the fireplace and gave it to the one who said he was Constable Dyke. He looked at it and handed it to the other policeman, Constable MacPherson. They both nodded.

"That's her," said Constable MacPherson.

"What?" I asked. "What's the matter?"

"Just identification, Mr. Blackburn." Macpherson handed me back the photograph. "She's fine," he said. I looked at the picture of Amy and thought of when we had it taken at the Sears in the mall. I couldn't help but smile thinking back to the way she always hammed it up for the camera.

"Your wife says you abused Amy," said a different voice, Constable Dyke's.

I looked up at them. I held the photograph with both hands and pulled it close to my t-shirt.

"I never touched her," I said. "Ever."

Constable Dyke licked a finger before flipping a couple of long sheets. "Maureen Blackburn said you sexually abused Amy on several occasions and that you beat her – Mrs. Blackburn – and the child for no reason whatsoever." The policeman looked up at me.

39

"I never touched no one," I told them. I looked from one to the other. They were both staring down at how I was holding the photograph. Constable Dyke looked at Constable Mac-Pherson and nodded.

"That's all for now," said Constable Dyke. He put the sheets back in a zip-up case and pulled the zipper closed.

They both stood. Constable MacPherson smiled politely at me but Constable Dyke just nodded as if to say thanks.

Before they left, Constable Dyke told me that there'd probably be more questions and to make myself available. I told them I wasn't going anywhere. I told them I was staying right here and waiting for Amy to come home. I told them that I took care of her. I'm the one who took care of her all the time. I'm waiting here in this house until she comes back.

"Thank you, Mr. Blackburn," said Constable Dyke.

"Take it easy," said Constable MacPherson. "Okay?"

All of that happened before Maureen came over looking to get some of her things. But that's not all she was looking for. She had a thing or two to say about me ruining her life, getting her pregnant and getting laid off. And how stupid I looked and I was a slob and she hated me. She had a thing or two more to say about my character. And she hated me more than anything because she wanted more.

"More what?' I asked. "What is it and I'll get it for you?"

She stared at me and her shoulders shivered. She looked like she wanted to scream.

"Stuck here with you and a child for the rest of my life." She spit at me. "Not likely."

"I'll take Amy," I told her.

"Not fucking likely," she said. "You put her in me but she's mine."

I CAN'T EAT much of the rice and corn. The egg has turned it all mushy and I have a few forkfuls and then decide to go to the bathroom and take care of my face.

I go in first with the light off so my reflection isn't so bad. I take a cloth and dip it under the flow, waiting for it to turn warm, then dab at the long scratch marks down my cheeks, over my eyes and on my nose. I rinse the cloth and wipe some more, try to rub a little soap in there. No question it stings.

When I'm through, I step close to the door casing and flick on the light. Back at the mirror, my reflection is bright and I notice how pale my skin is. The scratches are swelling pink around the edges with little flecks of bright red and dried blood in the scratch grooves. I've got gouges on the backs of my hands and down the sides of my stomach.

Slipping off what's left of my shirt, I turn and see there are scratch marks on my back, too. Maureen must've got in under the shirt. I don't understand how she could do such a thing. I wouldn't touch her. I couldn't touch her. I wanted to push her away, shove her just to get her away from me, but I thought of Amy and I thought if I put a mark on Maureen then that's all she needed to show the police. Simple. One good smack from me and Amy would be hers. That's what she wanted, I figured. That's all she needed to get rid of me forever.

"Amy hates you," Maureen lied. She was screaming while she clawed at me like crazy. "She hates you and she'll hate you like nothing else when I get through with her." That's when she kicked me. I remember it.

I bend down now and roll up the leg of my trousers to see a bruise under the hair on my shin. I think maybe I sprained my wrist too because when I bend it back the pain slices. I stand up again and look in the mirror. I remember Maureen spitting at me and I feel sick with myself. Go and get Amy, I say to myself. Go on, you stupid, useless, idiot. And I spit too. I spit at my reflection, then I smash the glass with all the force that wants to get out of me. Blood trickles against the white sink and I think I hear Amy crying in her bedroom like she did when me and Maureen shouted at each other. I think I hear it, but it's just something in my head. It's like I hear her now, crying for me like she did when Maureen grabbed her and took off out the door. She was screaming *Daddy, Daddy,* and I was chasing the car in my stocking feet, running down the road till I had to stop – gasping and about to pass out – six blocks away in a neighbourhood I didn't recognize.

AFTER PATCHING UP the cut on my hand and wrapping it in a gauze bandage, I check Amy's room. I look at her bed and dresser in the shadows. Her drapes are pulled from when she was taking a nap before Maureen came and took her. The space looks adandoned like that and so I flick on the light and stand there staring at the poster of the ballerina I bought her last week to put up on her wall. She used to watch the ballerinas on the television, on the PBS. I'd watch it with her, too. Those women leaping through the air. Amy'd watch them with a look I never saw on her face before. Her eyes were like they were frozen and she never said a word. Ballerinas leaping through the air and landing on their feet without the slightest notice of it.

I got her another thing too. It's a clear glass bottle shaped real smooth at the bottom and sloping up to get narrower at the top. She keeps it on the little white table next to her bed. Inside the glass there's a ballerina. You pick it up and under the bottom there's a key you wind up and when you put it down the ballerina twirls around in a circle as the music box inside unwinds some tune they always dance to. I'd wind that up for her at night and let it play when I turned out the light. It put her to sleep like nothing else. A couple of minutes later she'd be sleeping. I'd listen for her breath at the door. Her breath and the music together.

I can't touch the bottle now. I leave it where it's resting and lie down on her bed. It's too small for me. I close my eyes and the first thing I see is the ballerinas she used to watch. I see them leaping through the air but never coming down, just hanging there and smiling with music sparkling in their eyes. My legs stick out over the end of Amy's bed and my left arm is squat in to the wall. My other arm hangs over the side of the bed like there's no life in it. My bandaged hand almost touches the floor. It's open and holding nothing.

DOWNSTAIRS, I pull the cord for the curtains and look out at the night. A group of kids is playing spotlight between two almost identical looking houses across the street. I can see the beam like a searchlight scanning up at the sky and disappearing.

There's a knock on the door and I go out to see a little kid in a scout uniform selling chocolate bars.

"They got almonds in them?" I ask him.

He shrugs. "I don't know. Maybe." But he doesn't bother looking at the bar. He just holds it in his hand like he's on television.

I smile and reach into my pocket for the thin fold of bills.

"You in an accident?" asks the boy.

"You bet," I say, chuckling and pressing my lips tight together to keep in the pain. I try smiling but my eyes feel red and puffy.

"How much?"

"One dollar."

"Gimme two. No, hang on." I count the bills, my bandaged hand stinging a little when I bend my fingers. I've got two fives, a two and four ones. That's all there is. "I got sixteen dollars," I tell him. "My wife just left me and took my little girl. You know the girl that lived here – Amy?"

The boy scout shrugs.

"Amy who lives here? Amy loves chocolate bars."

The kid looks at the money, then looks at my face. I can see his eyes tracing the scratch marks.

"You're a boy scout, right?"

He nods.

"So who you help lately?" I don't know why I ask him that. I know it makes no sense to him.

"I don't know," he says.

I look down at the money and shake my head. A tiny laugh trembles somewhere in me but doesn't come up. I feel like I've got a flu coming on.

"What you doing out this late, anyway?"

The boy shrugs.

"You got sixteen chocolate bars there?"

The boy shrugs and hands me the small cardboard carton.

"Count 'em," he says.

"What you selling these bars for?"

"For a dollar," he says.

"No, for what cause? Something special?"

"Hockey team."

"It's summer."

"No." the boy shakes his head real confused and laughs. "Baseball team," he says. "For the school. It's a trip or something like that."

"You got eighteen bars here," I say, tipping the carton on its side.

"I'll take sixteen," I tell him and crouch down, count them out on the floor and carefully stack them against the wall in rows of four. I lay the bills down by his feet. He smiles at me. He seems interested and he crouches down too. He stares at my face, waiting for me to give him instructions like it's a game.

"You in a car crash?" he asks.

I start to answer, but a wide set of headlights curves in across the lawn and I look up and over the boy's shoulder to see Maureen's car pulling into the driveway. Amy's not in the car. That's the first thing I notice. Maureen leaves her headlights on and stares up at me. The headlights glare off the white garage door and her face glows. I don't know what she's thinking, but her eyes look crazy even from this far up. The boy scout turns his head to look at the car. The Escort idles and I hear far away screams of children playing off in the neighbours' yards.

Maureen just sits there, staring up at the doorway. The engine purrs smooth and even. But then it screeches and the headlights brighten as she stomps the gas pedal while the gear's in park.

"You know her?" shouts the scout, turning to stare at my face. I can barely hear him above the sound of the engine. "She's scary," he says, scooping up the money and nervously standing to hurry off across the lawn.

I rise from where I'm squat and wag my legs a little before slowly stepping down the concrete stairs in my stocking feet. Maureen watches me with her fingers clutched around the steering wheel. Her eyes are wide and white as black smoke streams from the tailpipe.

I step in front of the headlights and stand there without moving a muscle.

Maureen keeps the gas pedal pinned to the floor. The engine sounds like it wants to come undone. I'm not sure what it is, but I think it's the loose fan belt that's screeching.

Maureen screams behind the windshield and lifts her fists, pounds them against the thick glass, but that doesn't do much, so she grabs the steering wheel and frantically shakes it. Her body bucks back and forth like it's being electrocuted until her arms start wearing out and getting limp. Limp or not, that won't stop her from making her point. With both hands, she leans on the horn.

I can't stop the noise. Engine screeching. The horn drilling like that. White light blasts into my face as the headlight beams click up to high. And I can't lay a finger on Maureen. I just have to stand here and listen and watch and wait for her to realize what the next step has to be. How she's got only one other alternative left. Snatch hold of the transmission stick and yank it down into drive.

My Sister's Husband

One

MY SISTER'S child is two and a half years old, with a wild, dark crop of hair. He toddles around, thrusting his fists into the air and shouting senseless commands. I call him a little parrot because he repeats phrases that catch his interest. When I step through the doorway of their row house on Maxie Street, the child quickly jabbers, "Jesus Christ, da door," mimicking his father. The child stares up at me, his round face gripped by a scowl. He says, "Stash da dope." The words are slurred by the baby's loose mouth, but the idea is there one hundred percent.

My sister's husband is a biker with the Slattery Skulls. He sells grass by the kilo. People knock on his door and he sends my sister to answer it. She's his scout. The baby's a prop. It's just business, he tells me, overpowering my objections with a threatening stare.

My sister opens the door, listens to the visitor, then turns back and nods at her husband standing just inside the kitchen. Her husband returns the nod.

"Okay," he says.

The visitor steps in and the baby takes an angry slap at him.

"Randy!" barks my sister's husband. The baby cringes. The baby cries instantly. He opens his mouth and covers his face with both tiny hands as if expecting a blow.

My sister rocks the child in her arms and whispers "shhhhhh" until the baby cries itself out. They move into the living room where they sit on a green legless couch. A soap opera is playing on the fourteen inch television. My sister stares at the screen, rocks the baby and stares, enthralled by the deceptions of the rich.

The television is propped up on two blue plastic crates, the type milk cartons are delivered in. A coat hanger is bent and poked into the place where the antenna once was. The television's got a colour screen, but the colour's out of whack; people glowing green, their movements blurred. Behind the set, a brown curtain is drawn securely across the big window.

"Neat fucking baby, man," says the visitor. He pulls out a chair, flicks back his long hair and sits. Both elbows on the table, he focuses his full attention on my sister's husband. My sister's husband stares at the visitor, then looks over at me where I'm leaning against the counter.

"Go ahead," he says, nodding toward the back porch. He moves his jaw from side to side, waiting, until I turn and step out. The porch is a small, square room with two high shelves along one wall. The shelves are littered with paint cans and greasy motorcycle parts. A beat-up bicycle frame is leaned against the wall and a relic stove is shoved into a corner, barely clear of the back door. I bend down and open the oven. Numerous bricks of grass tightly wrapped in black plastic rest against the rusty grill.

"One," calls my sister's husband.

I grab a brick and close the oven door, step back into the room.

The visitor's face is glowing as he paws a strand of hair from his eyes and licks his lips. I lay the brick on the table like a meal going down in front of him. He nods and licks his lips again. Eyes glued on the grass, he shifts his rump and struggles to keep in control. He says, "Uh-huh," as if something's been revealed to him.

"Money up front," says my sister's husband, turning for the fridge. He tugs the handle and stands there, staring in. Ketchup, red carton of milk, and a two-four of Old Stock.

When he's through eyeing the beer, he gazes off into the living room. Even though he's watching something in there, nothing changes in his pudgy, unshaven face.

"I got it, man," says the visitor, indignantly reaching inside his jean jacket. He digs around back and pulls something up from his waist; a wad of bills, bound by elastic. Waving it in the air, he smiles at me. He tries to smile at my sister's husband but my sister's husband is not interested.

"No shit," he says. "You know that. Better than that, man. The cash. Right here."

My sister's husband turns his stare back on us.

"What?" he says, looking at the table, at the grass and the money as if he's just come upon it. Without warning, he wrestles his t-shirt over his head and tosses it into the living room. I hear my sister's voice, "Lay off."

My sister's husband laughs and wipes a big hand over the hair on his chest. Then he makes a muscle and squeezes it with his palm, smiles down at the bicep before punching it. Solid. Whack. He yawns and reaches for the ceiling, curses when he hits the pinnacle of his stretch, laughs and yawns at once, sloppily wiping his face.

My sister steps into the kitchen with the baby in her arms. She won't look at anybody, but the baby gladly checks everything out. The baby whines and reaches with both hands, leaning toward my sister's husband. Without word, my sister steps forward and allows the transfer.

"Babies are weird," says the visitor. He stares at me and shakes his head like it's the most profound thing there ever was.

"Hey, Randy," says my sister's husband, pushing back the baby's long black curls and biting his tiny ear. "How 'bout a beer?"

The baby smiles softly and slowly giggles. The baby jabs two fingers into his mouth, then pulls them out with intention, reaching for his father's chest and yanking at the hair.

"Fucking hell!" shouts my sister's husband. "Take this bastard brat."

The baby cries instantly. In mid-air, the baby is wailing.

48

My sister catches the baby. It is a natural act. Her arms are open and waiting.

The visitor says, "Wow!" and darts a look at me. "You see that?" He stands from his chair and scans the corners of the kitchen, searching for a clue. "Fucking all right. Flying babies, man."

I follow my sister out of the room. When she glances back at me, I see she is angry and frightened, but more angry than anything else.

"I'm working. All right?" roars my sister's husband. "Keep the baby out of here."

My sister shouts back, "Work your fucking brains out," as she kicks open the front door. The baby is in her arms. The baby is not crying. He's staring over my sister's shoulder and reaching for the house he just came from. The baby is in limbo; somewhere between brittle happiness and damnation.

Stepping out, I glance over my shoulder, in through the open door to see the visitor with his head poked out from the kitchen. He waves at the baby.

"See you later, superbaby," he calls, offering a stiff thumbs-up.

The baby giggles – bobbing with my sister's step – and waves back.

Two

MY PLACE is not much better than my sister's. I have two rooms, not counting the bathroom. One's a kitchen-living room and the other's a bedroom with a double sized mattress on the floor and a beat up crib for the baby. It's missing a few rails, but it does the job. I found it down on Barter's Hill at the end of Slattery where they were tearing down an old two-storey. I picked it up and carried it over my head through traffic. I took it for the baby, for when they stay with me to get away from trouble.

My sister sleeps on the mattress with me. She tries cleaning the place up when she's here, but there's nothing to clean so she just stands around looking.

In the kitchen-living room, I lean close to the window, let my forehead rest against the pane and stare down. There's a guy in a wheelchair parked on the sidewalk. I don't know how he gets there all the time. He's got no legs and no arms. A sign in his lap reads: Stop Killing Seals. The building behind him is deserted. Windows smashed all the way up. Slogans spray-painted on the walls. I read them all, dismiss most, but remember this one: Ego Is Not Art.

My sister steps in behind me and looks down with interest.

"He's still there," she says.

"That's all he does," I say. "No one around ever and he's there every day. Should be more concerned about saving himself."

"Yeah." She laughs with a slight wheeze. "You too."

I turn my face toward her and smile. Randy stares up at us. He says, "Daddy, don't go no where," and points at me, smiling slyly.

I tell the child my name for the hundredth time.

"Not daddy," I say.

"Not daddy," repeats the baby.

"I gotta pee," says my sister, heading to the bathroom. I check out her jeans as she walks. They're worn and smooth against her curves. Even though she's my sister, I can't help it. When she turns in the bathroom door, I notice the cut of her t-shirt; the cleavage and the solid sway of how her breasts are kept in place by her bra. She's been sweating and her flesh seems alive and inviting the way it rises and rounds out.

"Keep an eye on Randy," she says, matter-of-factly before closing the door.

"For sure." I look down at the toddler standing close to the couch, leaning in and slapping the cushions with his hands, trying to climb up. He keeps struggling but he can't make it.

"Need a hand," I offer.

He spins and holds up his arms without even looking at me. He just stares at the couch with a scowl and whines. Then he jumps up and down and whines louder.

"Up," he demands, huffing.

"What's the magic word?" I ask.

He shrugs and puffs up his cheeks. There's a dark look in his eyes that would make his father proud.

"It's please," I say.

"No," he says, stomping his feet with sudden rage. He kicks me and spits.

Three

"YOU THINK he'll come tonight?" my sister asks.

"We'll have to open quick this time," I say. "No damage to the door. I can't afford it."

"I paid you for that." My sister nudges me in the darkness, beneath the orange, woolen blanket.

"Yeah."

We are both lying on our backs, staring at the blackness above us that goes on forever. There are no windows in the bedroom. It is like a box. Randy is sleeping in his crib despite the sounds of a drunken man screaming accusations in the next apartment. There is no reply to the harsh threats. Perhaps he is alone.

Sounds from the stairwell also touch us. Quick or slow, uneven footsteps on the metal stairs clang up and down all night.

"If he comes, we'll have to answer it," I say.

"He's a bastard." She rolls toward me and I feel her breath on the left side of my face. I feel her breasts beneath her t-shirt as they spread against my chest and arm. She has taken off her bra. I am sure of it and even surer as she slips a warm leg over mine and sighs sweetly, cuddling closer.

"Thanks," she says. "Night."

"Night," I say.

I am silent as I listen to her breath. Inhaling and exhaling it seems as if my breath is guided by hers. It is drawing me in but then edging me away. It is as simple and complex as this: she is a woman, but she is also my sister. And I love her.

51

Four

"YOU'LL NEVER guess," my sister's husband said to me one day a few years past. I barely knew him at the time. "Guess what's behind that door?" A half hour earlier he'd sent a friend for me; one of his buddies on a Harley. I clung desperately to the sides of the leather jacket as we rode, sensing the thick emblem of the skull pressing into my chest as I hugged tighter. We leaned low on the corners, the sides of my legs skimming the asphalt.

"It's initiation time," his buddy, Nix, said, as he lead me into the house and to my sister's husband. He stood by the bedroom door, both of them leering at each other. Faint sounds rose from behind the barrier and as I concentrated I could hear the sounds clearly.

"She's a favourite of yours," said my sister's husband. He passed me his bottle of Jim Beam and I took a swift swallow and tilted it back at him. I knew what was happening behind the door. I knew about initiations, having witnessed them before. Submissions of any nature always enthralled me.

Nix and another skinny biker walked for the door. My sister's husband winked my way and grabbed hold of my arm, his fingers like pincers. The door eased open and we all stepped in to see two men standing above a white and blue-striped mattress on the floor. The mattress was bare and covered with uneven brown stains.

Three more bikers stood further back against the wall below the emblem for the Slattery Skulls. They were watching, drinking and watching in satisfied silence. The girl on the mattress had a blindfold covering her eyes, hands bound behind her back, every inch of her body covered with Nivea cream. There was a man on top of her, hungrily kissing her blind, pink face. The shock of sexual extremity began throbbing like a joyful bruise in my head. The rawness of naked, brutal entry – up this close – was overpowering. I lost my breath and heard only the clearest, most intense sounds; flesh whacking flesh and the popping of unintentional grunts; air pressured from the lungs.

The man on top of the girl pulled out and I saw her opened knees. She was red and swelling. With the man now away from her, my view opened up to a full view of her face. It was my sister. Nix tugged down his jeans and fell on top of her cream-covered body. Unbelievably, she was smiling as he slipped in. The other skinny biker kneeled down and unzipped his fly, laughing nervously and watching Nix rub the cream over my sister's lips.

"Get it ready," said Nix.

Laughing again, the biker bent out his shaft and pressed it to my sister's mouth, coaxing her. She quickly complied.

The Nivea was slippery over her skin and Nix's hands glided as they cleared the cream away from her loose breasts. He bit one, then the other, prodding the thick nipples with his thumbs until they beaded up and swelled in a way I'd never seen before.

Another first soon followed. I heard a sound that clutched me with its absolute, guilt-ridden pleasure. The sound was husky and lustful and overpowering in its absolute intensity. It was my sister's voice; racing, quivering as she gasped for the climax. I felt sick with the repulsive pleasure of it.

My sister gasped from a growling moan toward a whisper, "No, no more, not again, oh, god! I'm coming!" Her body rose, hips thrusting up. Taking the bait, Nix lunged harder into her. The biker concerned with my sister's mouth, suddenly, weakly pulled back, smearing his trail along her lips. My sister licked them and crooned, like a child. She groaned a man's name as if guessing. A few of the biker's chuckled, or shook their heads.

"No way," shouted one of them. "Wrong."

Nix pulled out as my sister climaxed. Body bucking, she shivered and her responsive breasts jarred and rolled to the sides. Then my sister's husband stepped in beside her. He was nodding at me, winking and dipping his gaze toward my naked, blindfolded sister. She was weakly twisting and moaning, spent but expecting more.

Nix elbowed me and then stepped in behind, shoving hard

into my back. One shove delivered forcefully and I was down and easily inside of her.

"No," she pleaded with a voice more pain than pleasure. But soon pleasure was racing through her limbs and she was thrusting with me, pushing, her groin up and rocking, her back slightly arched so as not to crush her bound hands, her face tight, lips pursed, neck tendons tightening and rising.

"Yes," she said, blindly bucking up and snarling, "Give it to me, you fucker. You skull kissing dead man.'

And I came in an instant, trembling uncontrollably and shivering into unconsciousness.

When I woke, I was sitting on the asphalt fronting of the house. My sister's husband held one hand to my chest, holding me up and he was staring at me with a tilted head. I realized I was leaned up against the concrete foundation. Sweat clung in my hair. I could feel it all over me as a chill rose despite the heat.

"Take you home," he said, straightening and standing over me. He smiled and pointed at his motorcycle; one in a row of many. Powerful sunlight glistened off powerful chrome, and I shaded my eyes but my sister's husband stared right into the glare as if it was home.

I slowly shook my head.

"We're family," he said, holding the bottle of Jim Beam in both hands. He moved his jaw from side to side, studying me. "Your sister and me are getting hitched." He glanced at the front door, swaying slightly on his feet. "I'll tell you a little secret, brother." A dangerous slur threatened to overtake him. He paused for a second, saying the words to himself first. "You want to hear it?"

I nodded.

"She's gonna have a baby." He offered me the bottle, but he didn't smile. "Celebrate," he said, eyes locked on mine.

I took hold of the bottle and held it, tightly, as if it meant something. The way it was almost hollow comforted and disturbed me. I thought of standing and crashing the thick glass against his face. But instead I took a long swallow. The bottle was more than half full, but I kept swallowing and swallowing. I couldn't breathe.

"Yeah, that's right. All of it," said my sister's husband, tightening up his fists in appreciation. "Now you got it."

Five

"YOU'RE GREAT, you know," my sister whispers, her voice groggy from the lull of sleep, her tongue sticking in her mouth, not wanting to move.

"I got nothing to do, except listen to the maniacs."

"You should have a girl here. I'll get you one."

"I don't want any women with tattooes."

My sister laughs, "I've got a tattoo," she says. "You've seen it. The little rose. You know where."

I freeze stiff on my back. Images of the initiation suddenly play inside of me. They are silent images, as if through my own submission I have been pronounced deaf.

"When?" I ask.

"You've seen me get changed before. Don't say you haven't. You watching when I'm over here. I don't mind. We're blood and I bet you seen plenty of better bodies than mine, right? I don't mind; undressing for men. Just skin. Tits and ass. I've stripped down at the club. I'll strip for you now if it gets you. I'll do anything. It's nothing, just pleasure."

"Don't be crazy."

"I will," she says. "You've seen my bod. What's the matter with that? A nice, cute ass. Go ahead," she whispers, teasing me and joyful in the game of it. "Squeeze it."

"Lay off," I say.

"Incest is the best." She pecks me on the cheek. "Night bro. I love ya."

I find that I am smiling in the darkness. I close my eyes, but it is just the same. I open them and make the smile disappear. I see nothing.

Six

A POUNDING on the door tumbles sleep like building blocks made of steel cutting into unscarred soil. I awake, clutching at something, but finding only the air. Things are falling on top of me, or is it only the sound, pounding into darkness.

My sister is still sleeping, or she is silent. She does not move. I gently nudge her; the muscles in my body tight with expectation.

"It's okay," she says. "I'm awake."

"Should we answer?"

My sister's husband roars; his voice wild and booming in the corridor of the apartment building. He kicks the door and frantically pounds it with both hands and feet.

"He'll wake everyone," she says. "The cops."

"I don't need the cops."

"I better leave."

"Leave the baby," I say.

My sister stands and I hear her stumbling in the darkness, searching for her clothes.

I hear the front door crashing in and the turbulant sounds of my sister's husband as he struggles to lift himself from the floor. A light flashes on in the outer room; the glow pouring in beneath the bedroom door. Then, with a rush, the bedroom door swings open.

"Fucking whore!" he bellows in the small room. He is a dark outline with the light behind him. He is a shadow that will violate the entire room.

I sit up in bed and watch as he strikes my sister. She goes over like a statue. I sit up straight and pull the blanket up close to my chest. He kicks her in the stomach, clutches a fistful of her hair and drags her crippled body across the linoleum.

"Bitch," he says. I stand and move into the hallway. I watch as he kicks her again. She struggles to her feet, scratching, shouting my name and the word "help". I look down at the baby. He's sleeping and I strain to see if he is breathing but cannot make out any movement. My sister is down again, stunned by a blow. Her husband seizes her hair. Face red and

KENNETH J. HARVEY

raging, he yanks her up, onto her feet. My sister's husband lifts
her over his shoulder and carries her out in her t-shirt and
underwear. I wonder about the blood within her struggling
flesh. I wonder how it connects us and what will happen if it
spills.

"My baby," she screams in the hollow stairwell.

"Whose baby?" my sister's husband shouts accusingly.

I step forward with hesitation, down the apartment hallway.
The sudden quiet is alarming. It swells within me as I stare at
the doorway without a door.

Stepping back into the bedroom, I whisper, "Randy?"

No reply.

I whisper, "Randy," and nudge him with my hand. He stirs
with his eyes closed and rolls over, away from me. My foot
pushes the bedroom door shut and everything goes black. I do
not worry about the door to my apartment. There is nothing
worth taking.

Standing here in the dark like this, I wonder about my sister
and her husband. I see them in my head, striking each other.
They are crazy with love. Crazy in the true sense of the word.
They are fighting now, but tomorrow they will make up and
everything will be fine. But for now, I will take care of Randy.
He is mine, I think. He could easily have been mine. My cock
recoils at the thought; memories making me wince. Mere rec-
ollections stir the body in peculiar ways. There is nothing in
my head but an ugly brain. So where do the images come
from?

Seven

FOR THREE STRAIGHT days I care for Randy. I take the crow-
bar from under my mattress and make my way over to Barter's
Hill. Randy in one arm, the crowbar swinging from my other
hand. People don't bother you.

The apartments on Barter's Hill have a buzzer system in the
porch. I press all the buttons at once and when a few people
answer, I announce, "It's me." and the door buzzes an easy
welcome.

57

Down in the basement, I bust open the coin-operated washing machines. Randy presses his palms to his ears because I have to smack the steel good and hard to dent it and pry in the end of the crowbar. In a couple of minutes, both my pockets are loaded down with handfuls of quarters.

I buy milk, a plastic baby bottle and diapers. I cannot afford new clothes, so Randy wears what he's been wearing for a few days.

"Pooh," he says when I dress him with the same clothes in the morning. "Pooh, pooh, daddy." He says, "Daddy, mommy come soon?"

I try phoning from the pay booth two blocks down. There is no answer at their house. I will not go there, even though I am certain something has happened. I am sure of it. Otherwise, my sister would be here. She would be here with her baby. It is her baby and she would be here.

On our way back to my apartment, Randy stops and stares at the man in the wheelchair. The man in the wheelchair smiles at Randy as Randy studies the chrome. The sky is grey but a pure white light reflects back into his tiny eyes. He squints up at me, "Kick start."

The man says, nodding at his sign, "Stop killing seals."

"Stop killing seals," repeats Randy.

The man in the wheelchair nods again.

"Come on, Randy," I say, taking his hand. "How about people?" I shout at the crippled man. "How about saving some fucking people for a change."

He stares at me.

"Save yourself," he whispers, his face changing, suddenly unsure of what he has said.

I lift Randy and carry him across the street. The road is deserted. People do not walk the sidewalks here. Instead, they huddle in doorways. I hear the words, "little child," issue from a dark passageway. The voice is filled with trembling joy, or is it longing? The buildings are splitting and chunks of concrete litter the sidewalk. The road seems wider and I realize why. Just recently, they cleaned up all the car wrecks – towed them away or dismantled them on the spot. The area is like a concrete ghost town. Old papers bank up along the walls. Coloured wrappers swirl in small whirlwinds. Ghost-like faces stare out from the unshattered windows. I read another slogan spray-painted on a wall: Silence means an empty soul.

Eight

OF COURSE I am worried for my sister's life. I should have stopped her husband from taking her. I should have cracked him open with the crowbar, or cut him with a knife. I had one in the kitchen. I imagined it at the time; lifting and thrusting it into his solid, corrupt flesh. But then I thought, in the struggle, I could possibly kill my sister by mistake. I thought of this, including: I am a coward. She was my blood and now my blood runs cold, colder. I shiver in the apartment. My teeth chatter. I imagine Randy watching me turn blue, watching his mother turn blue.

But instead, Randy wants to watch television. I do not have one. I give him three empty beer cans to play with. He stacks them and smiles when they tumble.

"You do it," he says.

I stack them clumsily and watch them tumble. They make a clanging noise that seems comforting.

"Now," I say. "Your turn."

The possibilities are endless; the things we can imagine to build. But I cannot help but ponder violent extremities. My sister and her husband clash around in my head. My sister dead? Two of them run off together? Arrested? Busted? Dead.

"Jesus," I whisper with respect. It is a plea for the mere continuance of life. "Dear God." A shiver glides up my spine.

Randy takes the cans – one at a time, with both hands – and carefully balances them on top of each other.

"More," he says. "Your turn." He folds his tiny arms and waits.

I gather all the cans from the kitchen counter. I cram them into my arms and sit beside Randy on the floor. I drop them and Randy covers his ears, but smiles at the noise.

We keep stacking the cans, higher and higher, until they

tumble. It is a good lesson for him to learn. Each time a little higher – a little shakier – and then just one more, but always crashing down.

Randy laughs intensely – losing his breath – when the tin buildings collapse.

"Fall down," he says, tumbling back and rolling in a fit of laughter. I watch him, wanting to be the child again, but I cannot hide my adult sadness.

It is from this sadness that I hear a voice in an opened doorway. It is behind me; behind my back or in the past. It is the sound of my sister, sweetly whispering, "I killed him," in that husky voice I remember and long for. I spin around, but she's not there. No door there either.

I face the baby. I listen. The building is soundless and Randy sits there, watching, bright eyes darkening with an image of me.

Kissing

I FIX IT SO I don't have to kiss anyone on new year's eve this year. I catch a plane, two days after Christmas, to Montreal, to this seedy little hotel I've always liked. Step off St. Catherine Street into a dark doorway and straight on up to incognito heaven.

The women in the rooms peer out at me roaming the corridors in the early hours. My dim form slips before their faces and they smile with the sweetness of a year's sleepless disorder.

They know all about "new year's." Nothing "new" about it. Just "years." Vintage stuff, this whole living and breathing thing.

They never worry about kissing anyone. They won't even let you kiss them if you try. That's why I like them. That's why I like it here.

I've been kissing people for too long now. Years and years of insincere lips wearing the skin from mine. Now, I just want to float aimlessly and watch the faces change.

That's all.

I've had enough. Especially on new year's eve with the balloons popping and all that booze. Another excuse for slobber-doe-eyed-loose talk.

I'd rather sit alone in this dark, high ceilinged corridor,

listening to the doors open and then shut, clicking closed like false teeth in a mouth that just won't stop, no matter how old.

I am happy, with nothing on my mind except the sensation of these people moving in the shadows, holding hands but never, never kissing.

Diagrams of the Brain

One

THIS GUY WIPES OUT on a patch of ice. His arms and legs go
haywire and it's funny for a second, but the main thing I notice
is the way his head whacks the sidewalk and stays right there. I
pull over into the slushy curb and shift into park. The car stalls
out on me and I leave it that way. It needs a tune-up real bad;
new plugs and wires. Maybe if I help this guy out, he'll give
me a few dollars for my time. He's still lying there when I
glance in the rearview and I remember what I heard about
people when they're down like that. You can't touch them
because you might get sued. The possibilty is there. You could
get yourself in a lot of trouble just trying to help. So I wonder
what I can do. What's the sense of even getting out of the car,
stepping out into the bitter cold?

Watching the strange position of his body lying there like
that, I decide to get a closer look all the same. I push open my
door and toss my legs out. Then I grab the handle and pull. I've
got to pull hard and push myself up with my other hand
because of the extra weight I've put on. I always pad myself
for the winter months. An extra fifteen pounds usually does
the trick. I go up from 185 to just under 200. I'm five-eight, so
that makes a difference.

Out on my feet, I kick through the slush until I'm around the car and up on the sidewalk.

The guy isn't moving. His limbs are twisted like the shape of a chalk outline filled in. Behind him, there's a playground covered with snow and across the street there's a row of suburban bungalows that're all the same except for the colours. I look at the guy and then I look up and down the sidewalk. No one's coming either way. The guy was carrying some books, but when he took the spill they flew out of his hand and slid about six or seven feet ahead of him. There's a package too. Something in a bag with the letters of a local sportsmen's shop printed across the front.

"Hey," I call, staring down at the guy. I tug my black woolen cap down around my ears and then slip my hands into the big pockets of my parka. I'm not wearing gloves and the air is so sharp it bites at my fingers.

"You okay?"

This guy doesn't move. But I'm not expecting much anyway. I spit off into the wet street and watch a car cruise by. The driver doesn't even look at us. I could be holding a gun or a butcher knife dripping blood and the driver doesn't give two cents worth of a damn.

When the car disappears, I walk across the street and up the steps of the bungalow straight over from where the guy fell. My breath's kind of heavy from taking those steps, so I wait a few seconds with my hand gripping the iron railing. I stare down at my boots and tap them against the concrete. The slush that's been clinging to them pops free. I keep tapping them as I listen to my breath. It's burning in my throat and forcing a flush into my cheeks.

There's a light on over the front door. I reach for the doorbell and push the little glowing button. Inside, the sound of two solid chimes bing-bong and an old-timer comes out with a newspaper in one hand. I glance down at his slippers because they strike me right away. They look like velvet. They're brand new; dark brown and smooth. The old-timer's wearing grey socks that're pulled right up, not a wrinkle in either one of them.

"Yes," he says, squinting.

I lift my arm and point across the street, thinking he'll get the message just like that.

"Guy over there," I say with a raspy voice. "Fell on the ice."

The old-timer looks past me, scanning the area as if he can't find anything. Then he takes a quick glance at my face before staring across the street again. He goes up on his toes as if to get a better look. Twenty bucks says he's blind as a bat.

I say, "Better call an ambulance. He ain't moving."

The old-timer studies me with his sad worried eyes, not knowing what to do. It's almost supper time. I can smell something going on in there. Warm food smells that're different from anything else you ever smelled, like those smells you only get a whiff of in other people's houses. I think maybe he'll ask me in to warm myself up. Offer me a bite to eat. But first his eyes check everything out. He starts on my boots and works his way up. When he gets to my pock-marked face he seems to wake up. His eyes squint and widen at once like they're looking into darkness, and he decides against me.

He says, "Just a moment," and lets the screen door shut. He even closes the inside door.

"I think he's dead," I call out. "Mother fucker!" But I don't think the old-timer hears me. I think the old-timer is on the telephone, slowly explaining the details of the situation.

BEFORE THE AMBULANCE comes, I go back over and pick up the books and the shopping bag, and put them in my car. I see the old-timer in his big window watching me and waiting for the strobe of red light to get there. It's coming up the road, then finally the white shell pulls up. They keep the red light flashing just to make sure everyone gets the point. Its colour sweeps across the ugly greyness of dusk. Winter is like that. Everything goes grey.

The driver jumps out and looks at me, then he looks at the guy lying on the ice and makes his choice. He goes over there, crouches down and touches different places. He tilts his head down and listens like he's checking out a time bomb.

In a few seconds, the driver straightens up and hurries to the back of the ambulance. He opens the doors, one at a time. I take a few steps to the side and watch him. Probing in the pockets of my parka, I find a few loose toffees and I peel away the wrappers before popping two of them into my mouth. They're hard from the cold and my jaw hurts as I chew, my teeth sticking into the toffees like sweet cement.

"How about a hand?" the driver calls out. The other paramedic is sitting in the passenger seat staring at himself in the mirror on the back of his sun visor. He has his head tilted back and looks like he's trying to get a good view of whatever it is that's troubling him up his nose. When he hears his partner call, he opens the door and leans out, scanning the area, then he climbs down and claps his bare hands together as if to say, Let's get the show on the road.

But instead, he says, "Brrr," and smiles at me as he zips his blue uniform jacket up as high as it'll go.

"Over here," shouts the driver in the back. He smacks the steel side of the ambulance with his knuckles. "For Christ sake! Get a move on. He's breathing."

"That's a different story," says the other paramedic. But he makes no motion to speed up. Two of them guide out the stretcher and roll it close to the body. Bending down, they lift the body like it's a sack of potatoes and let it bounce onto the stretcher. Once they've rolled it around back, they pick it up and slide the whole works into the ambulance like it's a huge pizza going into an oven.

The other paramedic comes out from behind the ambulance. He's smiling at me like it's a job well done. He shrugs his shoulders and walks right up close to my face with his hand outstretched. I offer him my hand and he fondly shakes it.

"You the one that called?" he asks.

I nod and chew what's left of the toffees.

"You did a good thing," he says. "Stay on our tail to St. Clare's, if you can handle the speed."

I PULL AWAY from the curb and follow the ambulance real close. The roads aren't that bad despite the lousy tread on my tires. My wheels spin a little, but then the rubber grips a patch of clear asphalt and I'm off. I try to stay close to the ambulance, but I'm trying to open the guy's shopping bag at the same time to see what's inside. With one hand, I tear at the cheap white plastic and lift out a rectangular box. I raise it up and see it's a brand new handgun. A Colt .45. A beautiful gun and it's heavy like it understands what it was made for. This brings a smile to my face. The bill is in the bag too, so I can bring it back or keep it and let it lead me where it will.

In between glances at the road, I stuff the box back into the bag. Then I shove the whole works down onto the floor in front of the passenger seat. I lift one of the books and hold it level with the windshield. I'm trying to glance at the title and drive too. This one's called: *Being and Nothingness* by some French guy. I toss that into the back and grab the second.

I slowly read the name outloud, Dante's *Inferno*. Crazy demon stuff by the looks of the picture on the front. I flip that one over my shoulder too and it hits the back window and lands on the ledge. There's only one book left and it's a real lunatic one. It's called: *Suicide Shots – How to and Where to Aim*. Someone actually wrote a book on this. Holding the hardcover against the wheel, I flick the dome light on and glance at the road. I thumb the pages, checking them out. They've got drawings and everything. There're sketches of a guy aiming a gun at different parts of his head and body and there's an explanation under each drawing telling you what happens – what the bullet will connect with and what'll be shot away. Which parts of the brain. Diagrams. They even let you know how long it'll take for you to die. They have it narrowed down to fractions of seconds.

The traffic light coming up is red and the ambulance is two cars ahead of me, so I can't run the light. I stop and pull a flashlight from the glove compartment to take a closer look at this book. They have different sections explaining the best locations to do away with yourself. They rate them by points, according to the neatest, easiest way and they give the best location-rating to a hotel room because a stranger finds your body so you don't have to worry about traumatizing the family and the hotel people clean everything up because they're trained in that way and, at the end of the list and most importantly, as they state right here on page 233 as PLUS #17 – You needn't worry about paying for the room.

It's creepy stuff, reading it like that. So creepy in fact that when the light turns green and someone blows their horn behind me, I drop the book and duck.

Two

THE EMERGENCY waiting room is a small four-wall box painted green with three hallways running off in different directions. The room has a television bolted up so high on the wall that you have to strain your neck to get a good look at the game shows.

Down at the front of the room a nurse in a little glass booth glances up every now and then to stare at me in a hateful way. I don't know what her problem is, but something sure as hell's just waiting to rip loose from under her skin.

Along the wall to the side of me, a man is sitting on one blue seat in a row of many. I glance at him as he leans forward with his hands joined. He's staring at the dirty tiles. He's balding and he's wearing a light blue polyester suit and a white and blue striped shirt buttoned right up to the collar. His eyes scrunch shut as his chest heaves with a sob. He shakes his head and another sob rattles him before he covers his face with both hands.

I look up at the game show. The big wheel stops on $400 and everyone applauds. I look at the man and see he's watching the screen too. His big eyes are pink and swollen.

I smile comfortingly and wait for him to look at me. But he won't, so I stand up and walk over to him. I sit down and he glances at me and smiles with his lips closed. Then a sob bursts through his lips. Only one sob as he holds onto himself.

"It'll be okay," I tell him.

His shoulders twitch like a shrug, but only half a shrug and he stares at the television. Someone solves the puzzle, just like that. Everyone applauds again like it's them who're getting their problems solved. A few even whistle. And the man laughs and sobs at once. Then he does the strangest thing. He reaches over for my hand, grips it and squeezes hard. He lifts my hand to his cheek and holds it there. Then he kisses the fingertips, slowly bringing them, one at a time, to his lips.

I let him hold my hand until he lets it go and meets my eyes. He wipes away his tears, then pulls a white handkerchief from his back pocket and blows his nose while he shakes his head.

"You look just like him," he says, reaching behind and stuffing away the handkerchief. "My Ernie."

"It's all right," I say, but I stand up all the same and move away.

FIFTEEN OR TWENTY minutes later, a woman doctor steps up and stands right in front of me. She has her hands in the deep front pockets of her lab coat and a stethoscope dangles around her neck. Her hair is real long and she seems like she should be taking care of soft little animals instead of bleeding humans. She has these full lips that are so juicy and sexy I feel like I want to bite into them. She tells me I can see Mr. Virgil now. They got his name from the wallet in his back pocket. The wallet that I should've grabbed while I had the chance.

"Your brother's fine," she says. "Just a bad concussion. Vision blurry. Hearing off, but that'll correct itself with the proper rest." She smiles. "A terrible headache too, as you can imagine."

"I thought he was dead when I saw him going down." I return her caring smile and try my best innocent look. "I was walking behind him when he slipped. He didn't move an inch. It was terrible."

"He'll be all right," she says, staring at my face as if to get an idea of what's going on inside. She says, "I told him you were here. He wants to see you."

THE LONG WHITE curtains are pulled around the other beds and I can't tell if they're empty or not. There isn't any noise coming from any of them so I assume what I assume – Vacancy.

This guy who I thought was dead is lying there with his head on a pillow and he's staring my way.

The woman doctor turns to look at me. She smiles and nods, she even winks before she steps away without a word. She's wearing white shoes that make no sound at all. Noiseless and beautiful. What else could you ask for?

I stand there looking at this guy – Mr. Virgil. His eyes are fixed on me and he turns his head a little. He stares and his mouth opens slightly. There's a black bruise on the side of his face. It runs from his forehead right down along his jawline. Or maybe it's a birthmark. I can't tell.

"Where's Cathy?" he whispers. One of his fingers is in a cast and he slowly lifts that hand, but then drops it back to the bed. His eyes jam shut and he winces.

"I don't know no Cathy," I tell him.

"My God!" he says, his voice tightening up. "Get her."

"That must have been some whack, hey."

"Cathy?"

"I'm no Cathy." I step a little closer and the guy's face stiffens. He looks horrified.

"Alan?!"

"Yes," I say, even though my name's not even close to Alan. "What is it?"

"Merciful God, Alan?! They told me you were here." He slowly licks his lips and the sound is sickening. "Cathy's in the house, Alan. The fat caught fire." One hand comes up and covers his face. "I can't go in. I'm scared. Please go and get her. She's your sister too. She's burning. Listen. My Jesus! Please, Alan!"

"Where're the keys?" I ask him.

"The keys?" he says, weeping.

"I need the keys to get into the house. To save Cathy."

He slowly reaches into his pocket and pulls out a ring of trembling keys.

"The address," I ask him. "What's the address?"

He stares at me without a word, but then smiles distantly, as if something's been solved for him. Suddenly, everything connects in perfect misunderstanding. He tells me the address. He repeats it over and over so there won't be any confusion.

THE WOMAN doctor steps back into the room. I don't hear her at first, but then I hear her breathing in between the sound of my breaths and I shift to look at her. She's been watching me. Her arms are loosely folded against her chest.

"How's he doing?" she asks.

I pocket the keys and smile. "He's fine," I say. "I thought he was dead, but he's looking okay." I think of the gun out in the car. I think of what he planned to do to himself. They'll fix him up in here and then he'll go back out into the world with whatever misery is ripping at him and he'll do away with himself. Or maybe he won't quite make it and he'll find his way back in here and they'll fix him up again and he'll go out and keep trying until the doctors can't put him back together anymore.

"Good," she says, sweetly looking at Mr. Virgil. "We're going to keep him overnight just in case. Send him up for a brain scan a little later just to be sure. He's still too disoriented for my liking."

"He'll need a few things, right? I'll go get him what he needs."

"Fine," she says.

Mr. Virgil starts whimpering a little so I step closer to the bed. I stand right beside him and stare at his face. I smile at him, imagining what his house looks like – if it's still standing and not burned out. Maybe it's a new house. Either way, I bet it's real quiet now.

"Take it easy," I say. "It's me, Alan."

The guy looks at me and his eyes are spooky. His thin, dry lips start quivering. I don't see any harm in being Alan for a while. I think of asking him for a twenty or whatever he can spare, but then he grabs hold of my hand.

"Alan," he says. "Did you get Cathy? Alan! Be careful."

"It's okay. I got her."

"You got Cathy," he says, smiling. But the smile is weak and only lasts for a second. Then he's instantly filled with wonder. "You went in there, Alan. I saw you go in there."

"She's fine. She says for you to take it easy. When you're all better we're going out for steaks." Then I throw in – just to help ease the tension – "On me. The whole works is on me. A feast."

"Alan," says this guy. "Who could ask for a better brother? Alan, I never told you before. I'm sorry I never told you before what was happening between me and Cathy. Love, Alan. Beautiful love."

ONE BIG MISTAKE. I never got his wallet. I should've gone for it when I had the chance back on the sidewalk. But I got his keys and there're lots of possibilities there. I even have the gun I need just in case there's any trouble at his house. It'll shut someone up fast. Just the look of it.

I saved him and I deserve something for the effort. He would've still been out there freezing on that sidewalk if it wasn't for me. I saved him from going wherever he was going to put a bullet through his head, so I deserve something. How much is a life worth? What do I get for that? In cash, I mean.

I go back to the emergency waiting room to catch the tail end of the game show. The guy in the blue polyester suit is gone, so I sit where he was sitting because the seat is still warm and I look up at the screen. The final puzzle is just being revealed and I curse. I missed the final answer. The big money's taken care of and I didn't even get a chance to have a go at it.

I push myself up with both sets of knuckles and step over to the front of the nurse's glass booth. Standing there, I catch a reflection of my wide, pock-marked face. I look past that to see the same nurse eating a sandwich while she talks on the telephone. She chews the white bread with her mouth open. A string of turkey roll hangs against her chin. She wipes it away and flicks her wrist toward the floor. In the process, her eyes catch sight of me.

I wave before stepping away, going back out to the car and coming back in to slip the suicide book along the white ledge and in through the hole in the glass. The nurse watches me while she keeps talking on the telephone, tying up the only telephone line coming in to Emergency. She reads the title on the side of the book and looks at me as if nothing much is happening.

I hold my index finger to my temple and cock back my thumb. Get the message, I want to say. But instead I press my lips in tight to the cool glass and stay there like that for a few seconds. The nurse just stares at me. She doesn't even shake her head. So I reach into my pocket and lift out the Colt .45. The chambers are empty. Mr. Virgil forgot to buy bullets. And that's one of the main things they tell you to remember. It says so right up front in the book: "Bullets are often overlooked. Do not forget bullets." It even tells you the best kind to get; specific brand names and what type of tips. Why would Mr. Virgil make a mistake like that? Maybe he wasn't serious at all. Maybe he was just toying with the idea.

The nurse watches me press the gun to my forehead. Her face doesn't change at all. She chews another bite of her sandwich and watches. I pull back the hammer with my thumb and tug the trigger. Nothing happens, except maybe I blink to the sound of the solid clicking.

The nurse pops the final bite of crust into her mouth, then she sweeps the crumbs from her uniform onto the floor. I slowly draw back the hammer and put everything I've got into my index finger as it squeezes the trigger. I do it all again, faster, over and over. Nothing. No bullets. No brains to come out and stop the trouble. Ignoring me, the nurse smiles at the receiver, at whoever she's talking to, and I hear her laughing and saying kind of loud and in a shrill voice, "It's the truth. IT IS!"

Dad

One

THE MUDDLED, LAZY beat of country music touches me as I step closer to his door. I read the apartment number, 101, and suddenly, clearly, remember printing that number on the envelopes I have sent him over the years. Apartment 101, Seaside Towers, Hollywood Beach, Florida.

Behind the door, his voice rises sentimentally as he sings along with the music. A smile spreads across my lips as if it knows its own course. It understands its link; its link to him. I raise my hand to the door, but I do not knock. I listen as he coughs and coughs. The music suddenly goes down low and he coughs louder. Then he stops and I hear him blow his nose before cranking up the music and continuing with his triumphant vocals.

I knock solid, three times.

The music goes down. I hear him struggle to his feet. I imagine his hands laboriously pushing himself up. His emphysema ages him. At sixty-four his emphysema tries to limit his mobility. But he will not succumb to it. He has written me about the dances he attends. A taxi delivers him to the hall. His breath – sometimes like liquid – does not arrest him, only slows his movements. He will waltz when the foxtrot wears

74

him down. He tells me he dances until he collapses. And I believe this woman-crazy man.

I tilt my ear closer to his door. I hear him stepping toward me and then stopping. I hear him fussing; straightening his belt, smoothing down his hair.

"Who is it?' he flatly calls.

"It's me," I say, not knowing how else to put it.

"Me who?" he asks.

"Me, your son."

"Blaine?" He fumbles with the lock. It clicks and the knob spins. "Blaine?!" He pulls open the door. He holds onto the knob and his face lifts with delight, arms opening to enclose me.

"What the hell are you doing here. My good God!" He hugs me with one arm around my shoulders, the other around my waist. He hugs me tightly and slaps my back. I smell his aftershave: Old Spice. It has been the same since I was a boy.

Leaning back, he looks me over. He keeps his arms around me and glories in my presence. He hugs me again. All the while, he's laughing. I feel the rims of his glasses pressing into my shoulder. I feel my arms not knowing where to go. I let my hands rest against the back of his white cotton shirt. He releases his hold, but then he takes my hand in both of his and shakes it again and again.

"Good Lord!" he says, pulling me in as he steps back. "You never told me you were coming, Blaine. I wasn't expecting you at all."

"I heard."

"Heard what?" He laughs and shakes his tilted head in disbelief. "It's amazing. You're here," he says. "Sit down. I got a forty ouncer." His thin head nods toward the kitchen nook.

"It's great to see you." I say, but I do not sit. Instead, I am overcome with uneasiness. I wonder why I am here; resolutions not being my strong point. "Where's your stuff?" He looks back by the door, scanning the floor for luggage. "Where you staying?" His hand comes up and straightens his glasses. There is a flush high in his face. He looks healthy.

"I don't know," I say. I look at him and see a man lying in a coffin. "I don't have any idea." I pause and lift a hand to my face under the pretence of scratching an eyebrow.

"What's the matter, Blaine?" He reaches out and takes my hand. "Sit down," he says, uncertain as the emotions shift. "Why the tears?"

Two

"SO YOU'RE REALLY okay, right?"

"It's nothing," I say. "My contacts." I blink.

Leaning close, he squints, studying my eyes. "Yeah," he says, pointing. "I can see them. Crazy things."

I smile and take a sip of my rum and ginger ale. The taste is detestable, but it is my father's favourite drink.

"Anyway." He laughs lightheartedly and shifts an inch closer. He is sitting on the edge of the rust-coloured couch. I sit in an easy chair across from him. A beige, square footstool separates us. "There's another one who says I raped her. Jesus Christ!" He laughs with natural generosity and shakes his head. "You should see her face. It'd frighten you." Struggling with his laughter, he forces out the words, "I said to her, Go look in the mirror. Who'd rape you." He rubs his hands along his brown trousers, licks his lips and watches me. Then he leans forward with a brimming smile and grips his drink from the footstool.

I look above him to a black velvet painting of a brown lady. She is naked and posing on her knees with her back arched. The picture stands out like life itself against the white wall.

I lean toward him and raise my glass.

"Here," he says, raising his. "A toast."

I wait for him as he ponders the proper words. His eyes shift toward the ceiling, searching. His face tightens as if he's reading something up there, then his eyes dart back at me.

"To a long stay," he says.

We clink glasses.

"You got a girlfriend now? That's one thing you never mention in your letters. You never talk about women."

"Women scare me," I say.

"You get them, you hold on to them. Hold on to them good."

"I guess that's it." I smile at this easy solution and think of Gary sitting out in the BMW, faithfully awaiting my return.

"I've had mine crated up for ten years. No disrespect." He glances down at his crotch. "Just as well. Stand to attention, you." He laughs and shakes his head, "Oh, good Lord!" He is laughing, but there is a sense of self-censure in his voice. "Shocking," he says. He sucks on his bottom lip and tuts three times.

I want to ask him how he feels, but I cannot think of a way to broach the topic. I find myself looking at his legs. My sister Sharon wrote me about his legs. Cancer in both of them. Cancer in his stomach. Cancer everywhere from how she said it. She wrote me to keep quiet. She wrote, Do not mention that I told you this information. This information was given me by his doctor who has violated his oath by relaying this information on to me. I do not want trouble. The old man is dying. You may want to see him. I, on the other hand, have seen enough.

My sister Sharon is not one to harbour pleasantries. She is over-weight and has been so for as long as I can remember. She does not bother dieting or improving herself. Instead, she nurtures anger and takes to gossip like a hyena to a wounded fawn. She does her best to pull the plug on the world's font of happiness.

My sister is a filing clerk for the government. And is married to another filing clerk. They have a house in a flowerless cul-de-sac. I have seen several pictures. She keeps sending them when they paint the house. Same angle; front on. I have photos of a blue house, a green house, and a white house. I keep the pictures on my refrigerator door and show them to people. "This is my sister," I tell them. My sister and her husband do not know their neighbours. They travel to Florida each year to vacation and visit my father for two days. They do not produce children. It is out of the question. Where would they file offspring? Under what letter and for how long?

We are not close. We are the distance of stars even though we live only cities apart in upstate New York.

I try not to look at the limbs of my father. Instead, I tune in to what he is saying.

"We had a forty ouncer a while back and some women. It was over at Cal's place." My father puts down his drink and looks at his arms. He rolls each shirt sleeve up half way, then lifts his glass, sips it and smiles. "He had a woman and I had one. We were just up there on the stairs coming back to my place and I had my arm around this woman and she fell. On her way down she pulled me right on top of her. Broke her collar-bone and her shoulder right here. She's just back to work now. I won't tell you her name. I won't mention it. No."

"Did she go to the hospital?"

"Sure, right away. And this other one." He tilts his head toward the wall. The ugly woman he spoke of earlier lives next door. Or so I assume. "This one said I knocked the woman down. She told people in the building. You believe that?" He laughs and swallows his drink, pours another. The ginger ale fizzes up. He watches it for a moment, scratches the stubble on his upper lip and then goes on. "This ugly one is always at the washer, too. The laundry room's right alongside my apartment. Right over there." He gestures toward the wall on the other side. "She's always at the washer, looking in at people's clothes. I said to her, What're you doing, and she said, I'm just seeing if the washer's free. I said, You know well the washer's going. You can hear it. You know well the clothes aren't yours. You get closer you can feel the machine shaking. You don't have to look inside, nosy bastard." Smiling, he leans over to pat my hand. "She's ugly. Oh, Christ!" He shudders in the worst possible way, closes his eyes and scrunches up his face in disgust. He sticks out his tongue and curls it to the side.

I laugh and stand. I move to the apartment window and look at the parking lot. The window is level with the asphalt. All I see are the tires and lower chassis of the cars up front. Further back I can see the full bodies of cars, buildings, and the bright blue sky. Up close to me, I see my BMW by the main entrance. I cannot see Gary, but I know he is there. He is sitting in the front seat, reading the cartoons in a tattered copy of the New Yorker. It is our vacation. When we pulled into the parking lot

I told him to wait in the car. I did not want him to touch me in front of my father. I did not want to explain to my father; a man who hungers for women. A man who desires nothing more than to share this hunger with his son. What else is there but women? He has said this to me all of his life.

Outside the window and closer up, a pair of slow legs step past. They are wearing grey nylons, but they do not veil the thick veins.

"That's Mrs. Craig." Dad coughs and coughs. "Her," he says. I hear the cubes in his drink rattle and I turn to see him holding up his drink and pointing with an extended finger. He coughs. "That's another nosy bastard." He coughs and coughs.

I walk over to him and lift his drink away. I rest it on the footstool. His head leans forward weakly but then he looks up at me. Shaking his head, he wipes the water from his eyes with the butt of his hand.

"That cough," he says with a raspy voice. I hand him his drink and he takes a necessary sip. "Had to lay off the cigarettes."

"No kidding."

"Just last week." He nods and wipes his mouth.

"Smart move."

I stand and stare down at him. I shake my head as if he's a naughty boy. I do not like looking at him from this angle. I sit and he squints and looks at the floor as if trying to remember.

"Oh, yeah," he says. He points up at the window. "Mrs. Craig. One day I saw feet standing by my door. The light comes in from the main entrance up the stairs and throws shadows under my door. Beneath the crack I saw the shadow of shoes. Two busybodies listening. I stepped over real slow cause I knew. I opened the door fast and two of them were there. What're you doing? I asked. She said – this one – Mrs. Craig said, I took a spell and I was resting my head against the door." My father laughs uncontrollably. "Oh, my God!" he says, biting his bottom lip to contain the laughter. He straightens his glasses on his nose, but he doesn't stop laughing.

"You're a hard case, Dad."

He winks at me and lifts his drink.

"How's your emphysema?" I ask.

"They gave me a mask and some gear that I breathe into for a while every day." He points to the side table where the clear mask rests beside a statue of the Virgin Mary. A photo of my mother sits on a white crocheted doily. Staring at the photo, I am filled with a longing that has escaped me since her death. I love her more than anything. It is the power of this love that weakens me; frightens and drives me into a life of seclusion.

My father's mask is attached to a small piece of equipment no more than a foot and a half long. There is a thin blue tube coiled beside it.

"Seems easy enough." I say.

"Oh, there's nothing to it." He grabs for the mask and pulls it over, holds it against his mouth and talks. "See."

Again, I turn for the window. I join my hands behind my back. I am slightly anxious. My father is here now, but soon he will be gone and I will remember this episode with a clarity that I am certain will defeat me for years.

"Not much of a view."

I look back at him. He's smiling as if expecting more from me.

"Are you staying?" he asks.

"I have to get back," I lie. "I just drove down to see you."

"Work," he says. "I remember that." He smiles wide and with the pleasure of confident understanding.

I wonder, What is he thinking? Why do they say this man is a dying breed? Why don't they make them like him anymore? Face your death, I want to say to him. Why are you so happy, old man? I realize this is my sister speaking. I try not to think like this, with the sense of cruelty that sometimes overtook my mother. I try to be more like my father. I will be my father. When he dies I promise I will be everything he had wanted to be. I will be him.

"So what are the women prospects like?"

I shrug and step back by his seat. I bend down and stare at his face. I slowly move my face very near to his. He laughs up close. He is not nervous. He is genuinely amused.

"What're you doing, Blaine?"

I lean in closer and kiss him gently, passionately on the lips. I kiss him the way I imagine my mother would have.

"Blaine," he whispers. There is a longing in his voice and I wonder what type it could possibly be.

"I'm sorry, Dad," I say.

"Where are you going, Blaine?"

I step for the door. I step outside and shut it behind me. I think of Gary in the car. We will drive into Miami and loll on the beach. Our bodies will turn brown and – in time – our souls will darken.

When my father dies, I will bury him beside my mother, and when I die I will be buried on the other side of her. We will all be emptied of morals and ideals, and set deep in this earth. We will all be clean in heaven.

I stand close to the door and hear Dad softly laughing and then coughing as the country music blares. As if nothing has happened, he joyously sings along with the sad songs. Dad understands the simple things. I listen and yearn to understand his death.

Three

IN THE PARKING LOT, as I back out, I see my father's face in the window. He watches, then turns away. He does not wave. Gary laughs at the pathetic face of the old guy.

"Did you see him?" he says. He is a brazen cynic and I laugh with him. He tells me about something he's heard on the radio, something about a forecast for straight sunshine.

"Unending sunshine," says Gary, then he scoffs, "It'll probably rain."

I turn out of the lot. We roll effortlessly as I search the channels, spin the smooth dial until I find a country station. I sit back, listening, expecting to hear my father there speaking to me.

"Perfect," Gary says. He claps his hands together, points at the radio and laughs.

I look at him. I stare at him. He shuts up quickly. Driving

81

along the straight road with buildings for the elderly on either side of us, I feel a nostalgic pang of love. I sing along to the music. Everybody knows the lyrics. I never thought I did, but I guess everybody does, whether they realize it or not. The lyrics lament the loss of a woman. Everyone could easily sing along. But instead, everyone pretends they do not know the words.

"What's the matter with country music?" I ask Gary.

He shrugs and stares straight ahead at the bright buildings pointing toward the bright sky. Old people everywhere are breathing the bright air and waiting for death.

"I'm just thinking," I say. I examine his clean, smooth face. His eyes blink. "What's so bloody horrible about it?"

He looks at me and shrugs.

"Let's hit the beach," he says.

I realize the music means nothing to him, nothing to me. I cannot truly feel the words. I switch it off and glance at the speedometer. Seventy-three miles per hour. Old people stand on sidewalks and watch us whiz by.

My father sits alone in his apartment. I know he has felt this speed before. He stares at the picture of my mother, but he is thinking of me. He lowers his head, crosses his fingers and makes a wish.

I look at Gary. He smiles and rests his left hand against my knee. He shoves his other hand out the window and waves at the scattered groupings of seniors.

"If they only knew," he says, laughing.

I stare at him, then I watch the sidewalk. I see old people whooshing past like grey-topped, colored dots. They are elderly and all alike.

"What's there to know," I say, and Gary roars with laughter, his fingers prying into my knee, squeezing viciously.

"Come on," he shouts. "Come on, Blaine."

I must do as he says. I roll down my window and wave.

The Passing of Time

THE PASSING of time, you understand?

With what's left of me standing knee-deep in the Atlantic, I see my son coming in from the fishing grounds. They got a catch on board, but I can't figure what it is. Could be anything with the way my memory is these days. Lucky to come up with my name when a stranger asks. But, some things I remember, like now.

Maybe you heard of me through the years. Morris Quilty. They said I'd fished the world's weight in cod. Me, Charlie Coffin and John Fisher, we damn near wrote the bible of this town. Cleared the land, farmed it, trapped and hunted, put the road in; one road running to three of our houses. Soon, other men fishing the coast saw what we were up to, and there was them asking if they could have a piece of land, asking us, and there weren't too many we turned down. No, there were none we turned down. They were poor like us; all of 'em with old collarless shirts and dark grey pants. We looked pretty much the same back then.

"Hey!" my son calls to me, the dory bobbing and gliding closer to the wharf over the other side. "You're gonna get drowned."

I walk a little further, feel the waves pushing at me like memories. The water's glowing green in the shallows like this but not too far ahead it's blue like you've never seen a colour.

Blue like the eyes of someone who's got the closest they could to your soul and set that colour inside you, forever. Blue and bottomless and rolling.

I built that dory my son is fishing in. His feet solid on it. George Batten's young fella, Bill, is fishing with him. I don't know what they're up to; what they're catching. I forget the seasons. The catch. Imagine me like that. It's a sickly laugh.

Just waves now; all the same but some a little heavier. The big ones pushing you back to remember. The waves don't change, ever. They're still as fierce and godless. Other times, they're like your father whispering things to you at night, and you are its child, listening like you'll never listen to anyone ever again.

"How's the catch?" I shout with hands up.

"Get out of there," my son shouts across the bay, sweeping his arm through the air as if to push me back.

The water wraps snug against my waist and I look down to the way it's fitted around me like I was made for it or it for me. A big wave pushes and, looking up, I remember in 1911 when you could watch the sealing boats pass right by here. I was a young fella, married to a beauty named Tara, and she was with child; the oldest one, James, on the way. Was only me, Charlie Coffin and John Fisher in this town. All of us with wives and John with two young ones already. We came down from Dog Island 'cause there was nothing left there for us. There wasn't enough so we loaded up and shoved off along the coast until we came to this place and fell for it like we were head over heels. We ran ashore and leaped free of the boats and my feet were solid like they get when you step to land after a time on the water.

Someone else is shouting to me now. It's George Batten's young fella, Bill, waving and shouting for me to move back. But I can't turn back now. You've got to understand. The old way. You start something, you finish it and no young fella's gonna tell you what to do when it comes to something like this. Like trying to change the weather, but the weather's inside of you and there's no letting up.

There's no sun today and I can feel the chill. I'm bald as a badger and there's a breeze at my head. It's rising to a wind. Maybe a storm brewing. I know and I'll tell you, yes, there's a storm brewing. The air is full with a storm. Smell the salt air almost wet with a mist, just barely though. It's the waves in the air, rising, invisible but rising. Fishermen see these things; invisible like they are, we see them.

My son is closer to the wharf now. They'll be tied up 'fore you know it. Safe and solid on the wood slats of the wharf. Safe in his house up there on the rock. The wind whipping, but him safe and warm with his family in the house we built together.

Another big wave leans me back and it's 1946 and there's thirty or forty families living in this cove and I'm the king of it all. I own the store and buy the rabbits and the caribou and sell everything 'cause its after the war and things are seeming all right and the fish are plenty and I'm fishing, too, with Tara minding the store while I'm out. But then the shop burns down. That's when it started. I felt the passing of time like the burnt skeleton of that store was what was left of my life, propped up before me and for everyone to see. That was the beginning.

Now, just look behind me. Look at the cove; big tin fish plant and those ugly houses built like rectangle boxes with slant roofs and fat clapboarding. Turn your stomach. And the snowmobiles and chainsaws and all that jewelry. But come what may, the water stays the same. I'm shivering but it's warm, too. You know what love is like. The sea. It feels like a woman around you. Up to my chest, it feels like the pull of a woman. The water throbbing against my chest. Water flicking my skin. Salty kisses lifting a smile from me.

With the water this high, full around me, I feel right strange, like it's the shape of my Tara pressing close to me. She died ten years ago and we buried her at sea. She wanted that. Said she'd watched the water so much waiting for me to come in safe from the fishing grounds that it was in her veins. It swelled its way into her blood the way she stared out to sea, and the only place for her was in it. She said, "Dead and in it to be at peace."

My son is leaping from the dory and waving right frantic. He's running and I close my eyes, tight. I don't want to see him coming. The bob of the salt water touches my lips and I feel the drag pulling, step four more times, feel the drag taking me under.

The passing of time, you understand. No need to explain.

Swan

One

ON SATURDAYS, Clarence's wife Ursula sits at the kitchen table clipping coupons from the *Post Weekly* and carefully recording special grocery prices on the back of a brown paper bag. Her concentration is precise as she matches numbers to the sale dates and locations. Planning of this nature has always been a necessity. Sometimes Ursula walks over half a mile – as she did last Thursday – to save twelve cents on a loaf of bread.

On Saturdays, her husband Clarence retrieves an abandoned newspaper from the L&M Take Out at the end of the street before heading for the park with the couple's eight year old son, Danny. Some early customer always leaves a paper lying on one of the white tabletops with brown swirls to simulate the look of marble. Depending on the briskness of business, Clarence sometimes finds two or three newspapers. The cook in the kitchen watches him without a word through the rectangular serving hole. He watches and then dips his head as he lifts a wire-mesh basket of french fries from the bubbling fat and shakes it.

"Fries?" the cook shouts, staring back up. His body-length apron is white and clean, and his name is embroidered across the chest pocket, spelling *LEO*. He dumps the chips into a silver dish twice the size of a hubcap, then scoops handfuls of raw, cut potatoes into the basket.

"No," Clarence says, glancing up at the order board's changeable black letters and red prices. After a few moments of regarding the sign, he turns to face the cook. "Okay if I take this paper?"

Leo shrugs. "No difference. I read it."

Picking up the newspaper, Clarence strides toward the back of the room where another broadsheet lies open across a chair. He lifts that one as well and holds both papers in his hands. His eyes are nervous when they glance at Leo, who is now closer to Clarence, but Leo is busy lowering a fresh basket of cut potatoes into the fryer. A cloud of smoke rises from the sizzling fat and is sucked into the wide overhead fan.

Clarence watches Leo's deliberate actions. The wiping of his hands in a wet rag. The popping of a french fry into his mouth. The sloppy chewing. Clarence waits until the cook says, "Take it easy," and winks before going back about his business.

The rich smell of deep-fried food lingers in Clarence's nostrils. Walking toward the glass door, he breathes the smokey aroma. He pauses and turns, leaning against the door's silver handle and pushing it open with his hip and elbow.

This Saturday, his legs wobble as he steps down onto the concrete landing. The newspapers are tucked under his arm, but they seem heavier than his entire body, so he takes them in his hands and carries the weight against his stomach. At the foot of Field Street, he stares down at the headlines. The words mean nothing to him. They are lines of black and darker black and even darker, thicker black towards the top of the page. At times, he recognizes certain shapes of letters and words, but he cannot interpret them. They are familiar, yet beyond translation.

Clarence pictures Daniel and the new words that the boy anxiously tells his father each day when he returns from school. Although only in Grade 3, his son already understands more than Clarence. The boy talks knowledgeably about computers and brings home an armful of books from the library every second day.

Clarence smiles fondly at the newsprint, knowing that

Daniel can make sense of the lines, make sense of the black, blacker and blackest. Daniel's mental progress as well as his physical growth amaze Clarence. At night, the boy sinks low on the saggy, brown couch and studies an opened book on his lap. The idea that the boy can actually see pictures in his head from reading words on paper baffles Clarence. Clarence has trouble understanding when someone else reads words out loud, and he cannot see anything when he attempts to decipher the words himself.

Striding up the street with as much brittle strength as he can muster, he is halted by a shrieking between two unconnected houses. The outburst startles him and he peers down the gap where two cats – one leaping into the air and the other crouching low – hiss and flash their tiny, savage teeth. The shabby cats tangle in a blur before bolting off, one after the other. Bits of fur hang in the empty air, then drift to the dirt.

Clarence shifts his attention up ahead to the end of the block where a group of rowdy boys are gathered in the road. Several are dressed in jeans. A few wear t-shirts or sweat jackets zipped half way up, while others are bare-chested. They drink from tins of beer and kick a soccer ball up and down the street. One boy shouts flatly to another even though they are within whispering distance. Their words are dull, their tones deep and monotonous. Clarence cannot make out the words, until one of the boys shouts, "Look, Debbie's fucking head," and swings back his leg to kick the soccer ball. The others howl and cheer. A boy of eleven or twelve kicks an empty tin into the air. It bounces off the roof of an abandoned car up on concrete blocks and rattles against the street. An older, taller boy – bare-chested and wearing a baseball cap – stumbles along the side of the street then stops. Unzipping his fly, he leans into a stagger, loudly hawks and spits before urinating against a fire hydrant.

The tiny stream collects along the curb and runs into the gutter, racing for Clarence.

BEYOND THE GROUP of boys, cars whiz back and forth along Slattery Street. A car pulls off the main roadway, into Clarence's street, and stops beside two of the older boys. The driver rolls down his window to ask a question. One of the boys leans in, swiftly taking something from his pocket. His hands move behind the windshield. Seconds later, he leans out and bangs the hood of the car. "Okay," says the boy. The car screeches away, blaring its horn.

Turning toward the blistered wooden door, Clarence pushes it open. He steps up and takes a deep breath. The smell of buttered toast saturates his stomach as he moves closer to the kitchen. His hunger becomes physical lightness – a desperate euphoria – when his wife places a cup of tea and two slices of toast on the wobbly kitchen table. Leaning sideways to check the imbalance, he tilts his head to the left, then to the right, before finally kicking one of the thin, steel legs. The blow does no good. The wobble remains.

"Stop it," says Ursula as she sits across from him, staring down at the thick fold of newspapers.

Clarence nibbles the toast and slowly sips his tea. He watches Ursula unfold the newspapers and flip the pages without looking up.

Daniel shuffles into the room, meekly silent. The toe of his sneaker catches in a tear in the blue and white linoleum and he stumbles slightly. Jutting forward, he clutches a battered tonka truck; a gift from his eighth birthday. Clarence had dug it out of a silver garbage bucket up on Freshwater Road during one of his midnight bicycle rides. The toy truck was practically new except for one missing wheel.

Clarence's bicycle is red with a blue plastic milk basket tied below the handlebars. In it he collects bottles, flea market junk, and sometimes, food, if it is in a wrapper and is not rotten.

Danny watches his mother awkwardly cutting a coupon from a large flimsy page. He spins a wheel on his tonka truck, glances at his father, then spins the wheel again.

"We going soon?" he asks, listening to the sound of his mother's scissors, shredding.

"Where to?" says his father.

"You know."

Clarence shrugs his sloping shoulders. Ursula glares up from the newspaper through thick-lensed eyeglasses. The left arm of the glasses is cracked around the tiny hinge and has been scotch-taped together. She straightens them on her nose and shifts her wiry, hip-less body back and forth in her seat. Her hair is a tangle of orange, neglected curls and her lips are chapped and open. Before settling still, she licks the tip of her ink-smudged finger and stares at Clarence.

"Don't tease the boy," she says.

Clarence scans his wife. He sips the cooling tea and traces the tendons and veins in her throat. The printed button-up dress she wears is cut low in the neck and the protruding out-line of her collarbone is hugged by her pink skin. Smiling, he shoves his tongue up over his front teeth, licking away the soggy smear of toast that has stuck there.

Ursula pokes her glasses up on her nose and snips with the scissors.

"Course we're going," he says, glancing at his son. "You know that."

"Don't worry," says Ursula. She looks at Daniel and nods.

THE PREVIOUS NIGHT, Daniel had heard his mother and father arguing and so this morning he is expecting some sort of change. When his parents argue, he always anticipates a little less. Things he took for granted are suddenly revoked. The hot water disappears. His nightlight burns out and is not replaced. The black and white television is sold. His recess snack is denied him. His food becomes plainer – a tuna fish sandwich with no mayonnaise for lunch, macaroni and cheese for supper and a cracker for dessert. The family will eat soup more often. He wonders what will be taken from him now – the trip to the park? If they take that away from him, he feels that the tears he has been holding in will flood loose and wet his face for the entirety of his life. He will run to school and never come home. They cannot take that from him. Fear taunts and confuses him, glazing his eyes.

Standing beside the table in the dim kitchen, he glances from his father to his mother. Clarence stares down into his tea and rubs his legs with one hand as if attempting to squeeze poison out of them. Ursula clips around the coupons without saying a word.

Fingers weakening, Daniel drops the tonka truck. His mother starts in her seat, jerks toward the small sightless window, away from the sound. Clarence looks at Danny and then at the floor without interest.

"Out of the kitchen," his mother demands, holding her rage.

Daniel stares at his father, but Clarence appears to be thinking of other things as he absent-mindedly moves his empty cup along the tabletop and continues rubbing his legs.

"We're going?" says Daniel. "We are, right?"

His father smiles weakly, his knees and shins aching. Touching the top of Daniel's head, he braces his other hand against the tabletop and stands. He is a young man of twenty-seven and sometimes – moving like this – he imagines himself rising from behind a desk like the man at the unemployment centre. Clarence sees himself wearing a suit, but his desk is stacked with papers he cannot read. He is mortified that someone will discover this and fire him, so he sits still every day, remaining rigid and wordless, waiting, trembling.

For almost a year, the counselors attempted to teach him reading skills, but after much frustration and an eventual series of tests they discovered it was impossible. A perceptual disability prevents Clarence from learning beyond simple concrete observations. This is what they told him. "Concrete things," one of the counselors had said, knocking on the office wall with his knuckles, "like this."

The counselor did, however, teach him how to sign his name in an uneven scrawl of big letters with wide shaky loops. His name is a feeble pattern to him and nothing more.

Clarence keeps telling them that he wants to work, but no one will hire him. He is slow moving and has trouble remembering orders. There are days when he simply cannot get out of bed, as if he is paralyzed by a dread that he does not understand.

"We have to go," says Daniel. "Have to."

"Okay," says his father. "We're going."

Daniel runs on ahead, down the hallway that leads to the porchless door.

"Soup for supper," calls Ursula. "Keep watch of the time."

In the shadows of the bare hallway, Daniel glances back – past the slow image of his father – to his mother, but her attention is focused on stacking the pieces of clipped newsprint. A second later, she raises her hands and stares at her blackened fingertips. For some reason she laughs at the sight of this and – for some other vaguely fearful reason – Daniel races back into the kitchen and presses his lips with childhood force against his mother's bony cheek.

Two

BEFORE ENTERING the park, Clarence bends down and fusses with the loose necking on Daniel's t-shirt. He does this because the walk has tired him and also to satisfy a need to move closer to the child. Awkwardness plagues him when he is standing on his feet. He longs to ride his bicycle, to glide gracefully as the sights to all sides of him drift past. But when he is with Daniel he must walk. The chore is clumsy and exhausting.

Clarence pulls Daniel forward and hugs the small body. Then he leans back, smiling with black-edged teeth, as if revitalized.

"Who's Daddy's favorite little man in the whole wide world?"

"It's me, Daddy," pipes Daniel. He watches his father, his eyes tracing the gaunt features of Clarence's face; the sunken eyes and the hawk-like nose, the stubble and the short straight, oily hair.

Clarence's stomach growls and he feels faint. If he stands quickly, he knows he will tumble backwards. Thoughts like the murky soup they will have for supper blur his sense of direction. He is swimming through the top of his own head. But something is drawing him back into himself; his pulse as a series of cannon blasts. Moving on its own, his stomach tightens and pulls as if cutting itself open.

Slowly, carefully standing, he waits for an inner reaction, then feels something tugging at his body. His knees crack and he senses himself tipping sideways. When he looks down, Daniel is staring up, pulling at Clarence's hand and leaning into the park.

"Come on, Dad."

"Don't ..." Clarence whispers to the whiteness tingling in his eyes, but then his vision clears and he is slowly guided along to the pull of his son. He sees the ice cream vendor up ahead and hears Daniel crooning, "Ice cream, ice cream."

Clarence searches his pocket for the shape of the coin and – between thumb and index finger – lifts out his only quarter and passes it to the ice cream vendor. The vendor takes it without word, then flips open the steel lid of the ice cream compartment. He is wearing designer jeans and a crisp, white t-shirt with the words "Poverty Sucks" flamboyantly written in sparkling gold letters across the front. With a frown, the vendor stares down at the child and waits impatiently as Danny's eyes move with gleeful enthusiasm from one brightly coloured picture to the other.

SITTING BY THE POND, Clarence observes the sunlight shivering against the slow silvery rolls of water. The trees surrounding the pond reflect onto the surface and the image is calm and soothing.

Daniel eats his ice cream with passionate commitment. The sun has no time to melt the sweet fluid and draw it down over his hand. The boy sits beside his father and studies the water, then looks out toward the clear center of the pond to the swan house.

"It's over there." His father points. The swan is hugging the opposite shore where a group of adults and children are tossing bread and cheezies to the solid, white bird. It floats effortlessly atop the water, suspended by a graceful buoyancy.

Daniel squints up at his father, then stands to throw his wrapper and ice cream stick into a nearby garbage bin.

"Where you going?" Clarence asks, but turning his head, he sees the purpose of the boy's movements and so he is silent.

Returning and sitting, Daniel says, "We need something to throw to it."

"He'll come to us."

"When?"

"Just wait. He'll come, like always."

The swan continues plucking food from the water. Clarence and Daniel wait silently in the calm sunlight. When the bird loses interest, it glides away and turns toward the father and son. The pond surface angles out and widens in an even trail behind the approaching swan. The smooth movements remind Clarence of the course of his bicycle. He wishes he could leave such an elegant trail behind himself.

Not a feather moves on the bird. Its long curved neck remains still and its delicate head is set with poise. Gliding close to the shore, it stares at Clarence and Daniel, and bobs slightly. Then, with little effort, it dips its head beneath the water's cool surface and reappears with a fish clamped between its black beak. The swan stares. Even the fish offers no struggle.

Tilting back its head to swallow, the swan's smooth neck jerks to the side and thrusts the fish onto the bank.

The fish convulses in the grass as Daniel scampers forward to grab its flopping body with both hands. Slippery and snapping loose, the trout arcs into the air and hits the grass before sliding back and splashing into the water. The swan turns and glides away.

Crowds of people on the other shore are calling for the swan to come closer, move closer so they can hold it and squeeze its soft perfection until their stiff, prying fingers capture its elegance.

DANIEL EXPLAINS the story of the swan and the fish to his mother.

"Just like in a book," he says, beaming energetically.

Ursula looks at Clarence, her eyes widening with amusement behind the thick lenses.

"It got away," he says and shrugs.

"The swan?"

"It threw the fish up at us. It did." Daniel anxiously peers at his father and nods for confirmation. "Tell her."

"Yes, it got away."

"The swan threw you a fish." She laughs, lightly, weakly. "Go away from me."

"Yes," insists Clarence.

Ursula shakes her head and stands from the table, steps to the stove to stir the soup. Thoughts of the swan tossing a fish to her husband seem unbelievably humourous. The image of the swan fills every corner and edge of her imagination. Its feathers could stuff a pillow. The muscles in her neck and back soften as she envisions her heavy head sinking into such a pillow. And right alongside this comfort, she sees the naked swan, featherless wings tucked in. Savory dressing, gravy, sandwiches for two weeks.

Purring as the ladle circles in the soup, her imagination draws the swan closer and slips a moist strip of its warm, sweet flesh into her mouth.

Sweet Jesus! she thinks, wiping her lips with the back of her bare arm. The swan!

DANIEL LISTENS to the muffled combination of his parent's voices. His father keeps saying, No, but there is an element of uncertainty to the weakness of his insistence.

His mother repeats the same sentences; the same rhythm — pleading, yet pressing at the same time.

The voices are suddenly quiet and there is a silence so empty it seems as if something whole has been taken from the air.

Daniel lies in the darkness. He stares across his bedroom and out the window to see the sky's dark glow. Somewhere the stars are shaped like a swan. He has seen a picture in school. A map of the universe with a swan in the sky. And a fish too. There is a fish in the sky. He smiles as if he is party to some great, joyful secret that no one else could ever begin to understand. But he feels as if he understands, even though he does not know what it is that stirs within him.

His ears detect whispering; his father whispering to his mother. His mother says something without whispering, her words stern and final.

He hears his mother say, quite clearly and with determination, "Think of Danny."

Three

THE NEXT NIGHT, Daniel hears the front door close later than usual. As if sparked to life, he throws aside the bedcovers and runs to the window. A small chair rests beside the window and he draws it closer before climbing up.

Leaning near the cool pane, he sees the street below. His father pedals his bicycle in the blue moonlight, effortlessly gliding to the end of the street like a thin, dark swan on black water. The block is empty and his father appears so tiny and lonely. Daniel wants to ask his mother where his father is going. He has a feeling his father is not off on his usual searchings. But Daniel is certain his questions would cause trouble and so he steps down and returns to his bed.

The sheets are warm and the room is filled with blue light. Daniel rolls over, facing the wall. He shuts his eyes but cannot sleep. Belief that his father is in danger unsettles him. A keen restlessness clears his mind. Tossing from one side to the other, he wants to cry out for his mother. He needs to cry out. But the image of his father keeps him silent. His small stomach is tight. With short, warm fingers he gently rubs it, then slips one finger into his puckered belly button. Pushing in, he feels a strange sharp sensation that puzzles him. It seems as if the tiny, shallow hole is connected to all areas of his body. He probes again, this time picking out a tiny ball of lint.

Staring up at the ceiling, he remembers the fish from the park. The taste of other fish he has eaten appears in his mouth. He opens and closes his eyes and pushes his finger into his belly button with less force than before until the sensation becomes lulling. And soon he is dreaming. Four chairs at a cluttered banquet table. His mother, his father, the swan and himself. Eating.

CLARENCE REACHES high and grips the dark iron bars of the gate. He is amazed at how easily his heels fit between the bars as he pulls himself up. Once at the top, he lets one leg dangle over, then the other. First he hangs and then drops, his feet making a quick, soft sound before he veers off into a patch of trees.

As if by instinct, he checks his pocket for the knife. It is a small steak knife he has taken from the house. The sharp tip pricks him and he is startled by the point and by the memory of him slipping the knife into his pocket with the tip facing in. It has shifted. Perhaps in his climb over the fence.

The pond's faint ripplings can be heard among the trees as he steps closer. The fresh sound of water in darkness sharpens his senses.

A thin asphalt path winds among the trees. Clarence stays to the left of it, watching for the guards. He hears footsteps up ahead, barely hears them before they are upon him. He freezes in the darkness, stiff, with his back against a tree trunk. The guard is dressed in a grey uniform and cap. Walking briskly, his wrinkled face studies the ground. He begins to whistle a tune but stops almost instantly. The beam of his flashlight is pointed down and he is scanning. Clarence assumes he is searching for dropped coins.

That's an idea, he thinks. But it is not possible. He has no flashlight and would most certainly be seen attempting that trick. He wants to turn back. Thoughts of Daniel overtake him. Ursula's words, "Think of Danny." The swan for Danny. But that is what he is thinking. His son adores the swan and this adoration seems to mean much more to the boy than food.

"They'll replace it," said his wife. "Of course they will," she insisted. "Think of the treat for your son."

Carefully moving on, Clarence's eyes adjust slowly to the absence of light. Within moments, he seems to see with a purer clarity in the darkness than in actual daylight. The dim, thick roots of the trees above the ground entrance him. The roots – as well as all of his surroundings – are brushed by tender moonlight. The grass is cool against his ankles and the blades tickle. He has forgotten to put on his socks. Finding this funny, he smiles as he comes upon the water. The pond is outlined by a faint bluish hue and he can make out the swan house in the center.

A flashlight beam brushes the water and Clarence drops to his back, remaining perfectly still. Footsteps sweep along the path above him as the beam skims the pebbled edge of the lake and continues down.

Clarence raises his heavy head and listens before sitting up. Bracing his hands against the ground, he lifts his behind, inching along until he is close to the water.

His eyes strain for sight of the swan. They search for whiteness in the night. The pond is a luminous purple, reflecting the changing midnight sky. Clouds are creeping in. The swan, he thinks, is sleeping beneath these clouds. The swan is sleeping. Of course, it is. But then a dim shade of white – more a grey than anything – startles him from the distance. Approaching, the grey whitens as it drifts toward Clarence. In the darkness like this, he realizes the overpowering size of the swan. It is huge. Its feathers are pure white and it remains motionless, staring. Then it glides closer to the shoreline and suddenly – without warning – rises from the water. On wide flat feet, it stumbles onto land.

A hungry, honking cry drones from the swan's black beak. Clarence nods. If he understands anything, he understands that sound. He thinks of Daniel and remembers the knife. Reaching into his pocket, he tightens his fist around the handle, then stares expectantly up at the sky. The moonlight is so soft he feels it is killing him.

A Handful of Change

A LOUD STUTTER of knuckles bounces against the front door. The sound rises sharp and clear into the bedroom, where I am in the midst of dressing in held-breath silence. I glance at Dale. She is asleep beneath the heavy quilt. Her short brown hair is loose and unruly. It covers one eye and curves down across her expressionless lips.

I look toward the knocking, then study Dale as I step across the bedroom. Her body is still, unaffected. Only her eyelids tremble.

Stumbling down the stairs, I pull one leg, then the other into my pants. The maneuver is tricky and I weave for balance, clutching at the wooden banister as I descend. A small blurred image wavers behind the beveled glass in the center of the door. Moving close, I see it is a boy. He steps back, then steps forward, knocking again, loudly and with determination.

I straighten my hair and stare down, surveying my socks. There is a hole in one of the toes. I cover this infraction with my other foot. Pausing, I tuck my canvas shirt in around the waist of my jeans before swinging open the door.

Bitter winter air presses against my face as if it had been waiting for me. It chills the back of my hands and nips at my fingertips.

"Shovel out your car?" asks the boy. He is tough and thin; ten or eleven years old, in a dirty beige parka with the furry hood zipped up tight to his face.

"No, thanks. I'm going out to do it now."

"I'll do it for nothing. Something to do." He is watching me with hard eyes, eyes that do not ask. They tell. He sniffs, then glances at the shovel balanced on his shoulder, the handle gripped by one hand. He yanks down his hood and his hair is short, brown and curly, matted in thick strands to his head.

"You from this street?" I ask, studying the feeble red blade of his shovel.

"No."

"You go around shovelling people's driveways for a laugh?"

He shrugs. "No, for money."

"I haven't got any."

"I don't care." He shrugs again, shoulders loose. He sniffs and vigorously wipes at his nose with a ravaged mitten. "I'll do it anyway."

"What type of shovel you got? It's heavy snow. Slush at the bottom. It rained."

"It's good."

"I don't know." I examine the quality of his blade. It is bent at the corners and the red paint is chipped along the edges. I squint with a question in my eyes.

"Which street you from, anyway?"

"Down there." He nods on an angle, off toward the beginning of my street.

"Where?"

"Stabb Court," he says.

"Oh," I say. "I see. Stabb Court."

"Yeah." He waits and stares.

I lick my lips as I scale him up and down. The laces of his boots are too short. There are several empty eye-holes and the strings are knotted in three or four places.

I check his eyes and he's waiting for me.

"Well, go ahead," I say. I reach into my pocket for a handful of change. There are quarters, dimes, nickels and a few brown-red cents. I count them against my palm, thumb bending to uncover buried coins. Over eighty cents total. I drop the change back into my pocket and look up. The boy is staring down the street, watching a heavy-set man walk in the middle of the slushy road. The man is dressed in a summer jacket and jeans. From the corners of his eyes, he glances sharply my way and pushes his hands deep into his shallow pockets. His legs move swiftly. Feet fitted in sneakers grey with wetness. They are the same color as the sky. Behind him, a telephone company van is parked along the side of the street. A man is seated behind the windshield eating an apple. Orange pylons are positioned beside the front and back of the vehicle. A young girl stands on the sidewalk, staring at the man. She is wearing a hat and her face has a sickly pallor; the exact shade of snow. Tiny white mittens cover her hands. She holds them palm to palm and spits into the snow.

"I'll be out to give you a hand in a sec."

The boy turns to me. "I'll have it done by then," he says, confidently. He smiles and spins, the shovel jerking on his shoulder as he steps toward the rear of my car.

I CLOSE the door and turn for the stairs.

Dale is standing there.

"I heard," she says.

"So."

"Stabb Court." She shakes her head, rolling her eyes as she steps down the final five stairs and moves past me.

"What're you doing up this early?" I ask, almost demand. I glance back at the front door, then follow her toward the kitchen.

"Day off," she says with her back to me, walking.

"I know. That's what I'm saying."

"I can't sleep." She stands by the stove, slides the kettle onto the big burner and switches it on.

"What about fresh water?" I ask, studying the kettle.

"The water's fine. It'll boil."

"I like fresh water for tea."

She stares at me. She stares and yawns, her arms folded across her chest. She's wearing a pale blue and white striped nightshirt. It comes down just above her knees and rides up another inch or two when she sits at the kitchen table. Her nurse's uniform is dangling from the ironing board beside her, waiting to be pressed.

"You watch him," she says.

"What'll I do, tell him to leave?"

Her eyes are fixed on me. She cannot seem to break the stare. Her face is wide and several strands of her short dark hair are twisted away from her head. She wipes her eyes good and hard, then looks at her palm.

"I'll go give him a hand," I say, turning.

"Watch for sudden movements. They killed someone down there night before last."

"I heard," I say, stopping, facing her, a sudden agitation rising. The defense mechanism – that is bred within – to sympathize with the less fortunate, to crush stereotypes, pinions inside me like a pop-up target. I wait there for further words from Dale. She is watching me with a severity that has not surfaced in her words. It is a questionable look; a dark warning. Her cautionary words do not concern the threat of the boy at all, but are focused on the threat of what is suppressed within me. I stare, and fury burns in my face.

"What?" she says, watching me, waiting. She shrugs and closes her eyes, then opens them. "Go ahead. I don't care," she dismisses me, reaching for the rectangular box of cigarettes on the table. "Just be careful."

I TAKE THE BIG steel shovel from the front porch and I'm out in winter boots, woolen cap and down-filled parka. The parka is brand new, with all the latest zippers and pockets. Velcro fasteners. I pull on my gloves and watch the boy's head rise from behind the car as I tug the front door shut. He watches me and I glance up at the sky. The low clouds are the colour of a dirty grey cat. They move slyly and almost without notice. The air is still, with a shadowed sense of foreboding. It is the settling of the storm or a restrained indication of what is to come.

I step around the car. The job is almost half finished. The top half of the three-foot snow wall left by the plough is gone and only the heavier snow – the slush and ice – remains on bottom.

"Good work," I say, bending and thrusting my shovel forward. I lift and toss to the side.

The boy stands straight and places both palms flat on the tip of his handle. The skin of his fingers shows through several mitten holes.

"Twice as much snow coming," he says. I notice his voice. It is smooth and lacks the fast cut of a downtown accent. It is the voice of a well-schooled, middle or upper-middle class child.

I stop and wait for him to say more.

"It's a red spot on the radar," he says. He smiles in appreciation of this dangerous colour. "It's the worst. The snow's usually blue or black."

"That's the new colour radar thing."

He nods, bending for a few quick shovels.

"On the radio," I say.

"Yeah. They said it was coming around two o'clock."

"Colour radar on the radio," I whisper to myself as a kind of private joke, too high-brow for the boy.

"Yeah," he says, laughing, standing with his hands on the shovel. "Funny. You can't see on the radio."

The sweat begins to rush loose when I stop. I can feel it beneath my woolen cap. It is rising in my hair. I scratch the top of my head and struggle to restrain my laboured breath.

"What do you do with all your money?" I ask, bending, lifting, tossing. "From shovelling? Buy candy and stuff?" I breathe through my mouth, then through my nose, my arms thrusting.

"I save it," he says, carelessly scooping up a small chunk of snow.

I stop and breathe, weakened as I watch him. "For what?"

"Summer." He glances up, tosses a shovel of slush into my neighbour's driveway. It's not shovelled yet. My neighbour is a cab driver. He's been out all night in the storm. I don't really care. He sells dope, too. His customers' cars are always pulled into my driveway so I can't get in.

Fill it up, I say to myself. Fill in his driveway. I toss a heaping shovelful his way. Bury him and all his uselessness. Classless, stupid scum.

"What for in the summer?" I ask, suddenly angry and disillusioned.

"I want to build a cabin. Me and my father, out around Holyrood."

My heart sinks when I hear he has a father. In this low income area I expect a fatherless child. My image is shattered. My belief in providing unequaled assistance to the poor boy is dissolved. I wanted to be his father figure. I wanted to guide this boy, give him helpful advice. Teach him. Teach him better. I glance at the big window of my house. There is only five or six feet of asphalt frontage to the curb. Dale is sitting against the back of the couch watching me. She sips her coffee and waits as if expecting something, as if it's television.

"My father has eight eggers in Holyrood."

"Eight acres," I correct, profoundly pleased at my sudden superiority.

He nods.

"Two years ago with all that snow we had, I made a hundred and eighty dollars."

"Really?" I feign surprise. Big deal. Who cares? My interest is suddenly replaced by a mounting rage; one of struggling with futility.

The snow begins to fall, drifting smooth and with certain direction. I look up and curse the sky.

"Just finished," I say, "And it's coming again, ahead of the forecast."

"What does the weatherman know?"

I have an urge to ask him what his father does. I need to know. Confusion has gripped me. I feel it in my face and attempt to relax. I pull off my glove and dig into my pocket, struggling with a fistful of change.

"It's close to a dollar," I say. "It's all I have." The boy looks at my opened, gloveless hand.

"That's okay," he says.

"No, take it," I say, thrusting the change toward him. It drops into the snow and slush. Several coins strike his worn, rubber boots.

He steps back, looking into my eyes.

"It's okay," he slowly says. The huge wet flakes spot his

parka and hair. With one hand, he pulls up his hood. The other holds his useless shovel.

"Take it," I demand. "Pick it up."

He leans forward, delicately collecting the coins from the slush. He wipes them clean and looks up at me.

He says, "Thanks."

That's better, I think.

"Drop by tomorrow," I say. "After all this." I motion with one hand, up, toward the slow snow flakes.

"Can't," he says, standing, turning and briskly walking off. "Going ice fishing."

Tomorrow's a weekday, I think.

"With your father?" I call.

The boy is half way down the street. He's walking backwards, dragging his shovel.

"Yeah," he shouts, turning and lazily staring down at his boots as he strides.

"Tomorrow's a work day," I shout. But he's out of hearing distance. Out of range. He's out of ear shot. I have more to tell him. Things about his father. I have questions. Why isn't his father working on a week day? I want to tell him about the people living in Stabb Court. I know. I've lived in places like that myself. I could have been one of them. I was one of them, but I made it out. I've changed. Now, I'm better. Better off.

"LISTEN," I shout at the boy. He's made it to the end of the street, moving off, then around the corner. I curse and start to run after him, but stop myself after two steps. I turn to the house and see Dale bolt to her feet, standing there, tense as if about to spring into action.

I wave and force a feeble smile. I see her lick her lips as I step closer. I am breathing. My heart is pounding. Dale is watching; her eyes cautiously following me.

Gripping the knob and turning it, I open the door and step up. I hear Dale call out to me and the sound is suddenly fresh and clear as I pull off my woolen cap.

"I was talking to the boy," I say. "He was okay. Nice." My hands are trembling. I watch them jolt as Dale touches my shoulder.

"I heard everything through the glass," she says. "You're lucky no one came along. Remember what your parole officer said."

"He was only a kid," I say, still watching my hands, wondering what they could have done.

"That's what I mean," she says.

My Own Bed

One

I WAIT FOR JACKIE in the prison parking lot. My hands hold the steering wheel and I'm watching the small steel door next to the big steel door. I'm waiting for it to open. Four months doesn't seem like much, but four months imagining Jackie behind bars is four million years in pain time. Her first break and enter and they lock her away for almost half a year. It'll be her last. She learned her lesson. I saw her inside that place on visiting days. I saw the lesson slowly settling in her eyes. The lesson filling in something inside of her that was missing.

I promised her folks. I said to them, I'll make sure she doesn't hit any more liquor stores. Locked away in the pen for busting a big window and making off with two bottles of Daniels. How do you figure that? Four months of someone's life for a window and two bottles of booze.

The sun is shining as bright as I can remember for early morning. It's hot inside the car but I don't want to roll down the windows. I don't like the feel of this parking lot or the look of the big grey wall with the watchtower ahead of me. They got guns up there. A lousy prison like this with petty thieves and they got guns up there.

I see a guard move around in that tower; then, far below the guard, I see the steel door swing open, but Jackie doesn't come out. Someone else comes out. It's a thin, balding man and he's smoking a cigarette. He doesn't bother stopping. He just keeps walking. He doesn't look anywhere but down. There's no one waiting for him. Nothing. He knows it. I watch him pass close to the car. I watch him push his thick-rimmed glasses up on his nose. He doesn't see me. He's too busy looking down. I think maybe he's watching his feet, enthralled by the way that they move so easy. I hear him cough real close but muffled through the glass, and then he's gone.

Someone taps on the window and I almost jump out of my skin. I'm nervous. No sleep last night knowing Jackie was out today. And it's her; it's Jackie standing next to me. I start to roll down the window but then I stop and go for the handle. I'm out with her in my arms, and I'm feeling her solid and soft against me. Her laughing and kissing as I spin her around. Me forcing the words from beneath her tight hugging arms, "How's it feel to be out?"

THE SWEAT IS ALL over us. She can't wait. Her hands are everywhere while I'm driving. Her touch is an instant hard-on. The look in her eyes is an instant hard-on. The closeness of her, the smell of her, the simple moving of her fingers as they light up a cigarette and then move for me is an instant hard-on. Then she's all over me, leaning down and slowly unzipping my fly, humming the national anthem with true enthusiasm. She takes me in her mouth, slowly, savouring, then leans up straight to devour a draw from her cigarette, smiles, leans down again and starts in, humming and blowing smoke out through her nose.

"Hold on," I say. I want to hold back. "Wait till we get home."

She leans up and looks at me.

"Where are we going?" she demands.

"My place."

"No. My place."

"Your place is a dump."

"Look." She is suddenly hostile. I'm not sure if she's joking or if it's the real thing. "My place. I wanna see my place." She paws a tangle of brown hair away from her narrow, freckled face.

"I wanna fuck in my bed. Then I wanna sleep," she says. "I wanna sleep in my bed. Alone." She calms down and looks at her fingers, as if imagining something, something she's touched in prison. She wipes her hands on her jeans and pleads, "I just have to, baby." Crooning, "Please."

THE DOOR IS UNLOCKED. There's nothing much worth stealing. Someone has been in her place and left empty beer cans on the table and floor. They've left burger wrappers and chicken bones all over the place, too. Jackie doesn't say much about this. She just moves around, looking at things, looking at things and sniffing the air.

She turns back to face me as if to say something, but struggles with what it is and then just shakes her head and laughs. Then she hurries to me with this really apologetic swagger and takes both my hands. She leans close. She rests her head on my shoulder and I run both hands through her curly hair. Lifting away, she stares at me with sadness. Tears come. They spill from Jackie and then they flow over to me.

"What's the matter?" I ask, but it's as if I'm asking myself. There is no answer and I don't wait for one.

Jackie steps back from me, wiping at her eyes.

"Things happen in there," she says. I know what's coming next. I see the tenderness in her face before the words surface. She needs something to help her forget. This will be her excuse. She takes another step back, fearing something.

"Let's go for a drink," she says. "Hm? How about it, Max?"

I stare at her and she sees the hurt in my eyes.

"Not right now," she says. "Not this instant. Of course, you know what I meant." She hugs me tightly, her arms around my neck.

"Oh, my God," she says. "Oh, Christ! I want you in me so bad."

JACKIE STANDS back-on in the doorway at the end of the hall. It's her bedroom and there's no door on the hinges. I watch her slowly pull off her turtle-neck. I watch her fingers move around swiftly to unclip her bra. I catch a flash of the fleshy curve of a breast as she leans forward to pull off her slip-ons. She's not wearing socks. Her fingers go round front, fumble with the button of her jeans. I watch her right elbow descend as she pulls down the zipper. I watch all of this, each tiny action connecting to a purpose. She moves without looking back at me. All the while, she's just staring at her bed.

I undress real quick as I step toward her. She turns to me and the feel of flesh to flesh forces us closer. I rub both hands down her smooth back and she squeezes my behind. We move like that, until I turn to the bed and take one of her hands, pull her down. She's on top of me. She's on top of me and she's crazy for it.

"Come on," she says, whispering with her teeth clamped together. "Oh, Max. I'm soaking wet. Slip in. Quick. I can't take it. Max. Oh, God. Max." Both palms pressed to the sheets, one hand on either side of me, she moans and watches her fingers. Her breasts are swaying wildly as she thrusts. I take hold of them and stare at her face, but she's not looking at me. She's watching her fingers move. She's watching her fingers clutch the sheets and push into the soft, soft mattress.

"FOR ME," she says, "Please. I can't explain it. I just need to be." She shakes her head and licks at her lips, then takes a draw. I'm out in the hallway, pulling on my underwear, searching for my other sock. She's sitting in bed. I can see her. She's looking at the walls. She staring at things on the top of the battered dresser. Her eyes scan the objects; a deodorant tin, an empty cola bottle, a pair of torn black nylons, a grey hairbrush with clots of her hair still lodged in the sharp bristles. Smiling, she looks at the beige woolen blanket pinned up over the window. She takes a draw from her cigarette as her eyes keep moving like she's at a museum and everything is totally fascinating and gleaming with pricelessness.

I wonder about the drink she wanted. I wonder about that. I want to mention it just to get her out of this dump, but I let it lie. I'd rather have her here in this rat trap stinking of mildew than drunk and stuck in prison.

"When do you want me to come back?" I ask. I don't know why but I ask it. I ask in an almost pitiful way.

"Oh, God!" she shrieks, jumping from bed and throwing her arms around me. "I didn't mean it like that. Just tonight. That's all. Not like that. Just alone tonight. My own bed. I'm sorry. I didn't mean it like that at all, Max. I really didn't."

Two

"HOME IS where the heart is," says John. He's short and plump with red hair and a red face. His voice is raspy. He works at an auto supply store. On his time off he drinks beer. He likes to drink beer and play pool. Who doesn't?

John takes a swig and stands, tugging at his pants with one hand. He taps the tip of his Palmer cue against the pool table as he wades around, surveying possible shots.

I lift the large murky glass of tonic water to my lips. The taste is sweet and bitter. I like the taste. You get used to it; sweet and bitter at once, like the feel of sex still on me, but the sense of defeat there, too.

John shoots fast. I hear him breathe from where I'm sitting. He labours around the table making shots.

"Slow it down," I say to him. He looks my way and nods, leaning and stretching over the table. The cue slides between his fingers, but suddenly pops up, lifting from his bridge. "Damn," he says, shaking his head, tugging on his pants and moving next to me.

"That was a tough one, John."

"Hard to get a good grip." He shakes his head and stares at the pool table, then sits with resignation when the guy he's playing pockets a ball.

"Sold the farm," I say to him.

"What can you do, Max." He shrugs his shoulders. "But what about Jackie? You say she's out and sleeping alone." His tiny eyes flash. He forces a crooked, almost embarrassed smile. His teeth are clamped together the way they always are when he smiles. He looks childlike, sweet, compassionate. He looks wounded. He has the charm of a fat kid who's taken too many punches.

"Said she wanted to sleep in her own bed."

"Maybe she's okay." John shrugs and smiles. His eyes are glassy. "Her own place. Freedom," he says as if it's simple. "Hey, it must be nice to get out of prison. It must feel like nothing else."

"Being alone like that, you'd think she'd want to sleep with me."

"Maybe she wasn't sleeping alone." John gives me that embarrassed smile. "Joking, Max." When he sees the look on my face, he reaches across the table and slaps my arm. "Just joking."

"I should see her."

Someone yells John's name. He looks that way.

"Whose shot?" he asks, a cigarette clamped between his teeth as he stands, tugs his pants and moves forward.

I stand too.

"See you John. Thanks."

He looks up from the shot, "Yeah, see you Max." Then his eyes dip down to find a line between the white ball and the black ball; the final shot, the black ball hanging over the pocket waiting to drop. A giveaway. But then I hear the sound of two balls dropping and John cursing.

I'm tempted to look back, but I don't. I know the feeling of eyes upon you when you've just lost something you thought was yours.

THE DOOR is unlocked. I open it quietly and step in. It's almost two in the morning. The place is dark, but down the hallway a light shines from the bathroom. I see Jackie's bed in the distance. I see the rumpled sheets. The living room window is open. Voices drift up as cool as the summer night. A car passes on tires that sound almost wet.

I walk closer to Jackie's bed. My body moves with my mind. They seem strangely in sync. The sounds fade as I step down the hallway. I glance into the bathroom and see the rust lines in the toilet bowl, the cracked mirror above the cracked sink.

Looking toward Jackie's bed, I see it's empty. I feared as much. She's out. But where. I don't want to think. I step into her dark bedroom. The air smells of her. I look at the window and see the woolen blanket has been taken down, but the sky is dark, no stars. No streetlights close by. It's a frightening view; the sky like that.

I sit on the bed and then I lie back and let my head sink into the shape of Jackie's head left against the pillow. She was looking out the window. She was looking at this black view.

I roll to the other side and stare up at the peeling dark green wallpaper. There are images of lions, elephants and zebras. It's not wallpaper for a child. It's serious stuff; the real thing. Real animals, watching me. I roll back to a view of the sky. My fingers move along the cool sheets. My fingers push into the mattress springs, giving rise to an erection. I smell Jackie. I sense her image in the room. I sense her weight against the springs of the bed, but she's not here.

Unbuttoning my jeans, I think of her. I grip myself with one hand and stroke the cool sheet with the other. In closer to my body, I sense the warm spot from where she had been resting. I touch her warmth. I caress her bed and I caress myself.

Where the fuck are you, Jackie? You move from prison into freedom into the trap of booze. There's a false glow of understanding when you're drunk. You think you're freer, but it's a strained freedom. You have to force yourself through that small opening in the bottle as you continuously climb in and out.

Three

THE SKY HAS CLEARED and it's light. I hear a hand on the door and Jackie walks in. She sighs and watches the door as she closes it. She takes off her jean jacket and tosses it on the ragged couch.

Looking up, she stares down the hallway and sees me. A smile lifts her face, brings it back to life.

I wonder. I wonder about her.

"What're you doing here," she says, moving down the hall.

"Waiting for you," I snap.

"Look." She stops. Her face darkens. "Don't." Lips pressed together, she steps into the room. "You know where I was?" She is steady and stable. She has not been drinking. I am silent. I lick my lips. I wait.

Smiling, she shakes her head. She covers her face with one hand and laughs.

"I was at your place," she says. "Waiting for you. I was lying on your bed all night but I didn't get any sleep." She looks up. "I was worried sick. I thought you'd gone off with someone. I thought." She shakes her head, struggling with heavy, exhausted thoughts. "I don't know." She looks at me and realizes what I must've been thinking, what I was thinking.

"Funny, hey. You in my bed and me in yours."

"I was watching the sky," I say.

"It was something else," she says, knowing instantly what I'm talking about. "It just seemed to be dragging me in. I stared at it and stared." She sits on the edge of the bed and lights a cigarette, waves the smoke away from me. "Sorry," she says. I lean to her. I touch her hair.

"I wanted you so bad last night," she says. "I cried and cried and cursed myself for this stupid bed. Alone. I don't know why I wanted to be alone. I don't know." Shaking her head, she takes a draw. She waves the smoke away.

"I know." I say. "I understand."

"Tell me, what is it?"

"I just know. It's like that." I keep touching her hair, hooking it behind her ears and unhooking it.

"I know," she says. "It's something inside, isn't it. You know. You're always good with those inside things."

I lean foward and kiss her. I look to the clearing sky and see that she's looking there too.

"It's funny," I say. "Me and you in your bed like this."

Jackie laughs and I squint, trying to understand the humour.

Its meaning evades me although I seemed to sense it only seconds ago.

"Let's get out of here," I say, placing a palm on each cheek. "Let's go to my place."

Jackie shudders, "I was there all night."

"I can't stay here," I say.

She lies back across the bed, across my legs and watches me.

"Let's just close our eyes," she says and she closes hers and I watch her for a while then close mine and imagine my bed with her sleeping there in the clean sheets, alone. I open my eyes and see she's watching me. She wants to tell me something.

"What was it like in prison?" I ask, not wanting to bring her back to that, but having to. Needing to know what she's been feeling so I can feel it too.

"Like last night," she says instantly, her perception sharp from fatigue. "Like last night, every night and every day. Sleeping in someone else's bed and waiting."

How We Sup Upon This Misery

THERE ARE MOMENTS between the drab heat when it rains, yet in instants the wet streets quickly dry from black to faded grey and the humidity thickens. Air molecules swell and, seemingly, press against the skin.

These rainy moments – briefly cleansing the stale air – lead to thoughts along this line: There are incidents of joy between unrelenting periods of misery. Or so I have heard. The fortunate are quick with stories of excess, whereas the stricken know no avenues of expression. Words forsake the stricken. Their tongues are not tamed by the manners of privileged education. What they have are bodies. They have bodies to keep themselves warm. Warm, soiled bodies; wiry and strangely agile, or plump and pasty from ingesting empty food. They stand in sparsely furnished rooms that stink of rot. Movement requires intention and so their positions remain unchanged. Set behind bleary plexi-glass windows, they stare out to view the scenery, hazy like a smear of dream juice gone grey.

I see a child lifted to this view. A tiny body rises, held by feeble hands. The toddler laughs. The face – man or woman – smiles, toothless with extreme love.

Leaning in my doorway, I shut my eyes from the strain and listen to screaming three or four doors down. Tires are also screeching. Two cars accelerate up and down this one way known as Field Street.

Behind me, further back in my house, my wife Pam is sitting at the kitchen table. She shouts, "Forget it." as a stamp of finality, sealing our prior argument.

"Of course," I whisper to her with my eyes still closed. I whisper this way, knowing she will never hear. "What else, but forget it."

Opening my eyes, I gaze up, across the narrow asphalt. I scan each window of the row houses. Above the windows, electrical wires hang like clotheslines connecting one side of the street to the other. The house across from me is black with white trim. The one beside that is pale blue. The one beside that – white. The one beside that – beige …

I choose one and count the narrow strips of clapboard. Listen. The screaming is wearing itself out, fading. It was the shrill cry of a girl. Perhaps it was a game, or perhaps it was the real thing. Definition wavers in a neighbourhood such as this. One scream is much like the other. Sickly laughter sometimes follows, regardless of the intention. There is a narrow, seamless division between the substance of terror and laughter.

Pam's chair scrapes away from the table and her quick footsteps sound against the kitchen linoleum, then are silent as she steps onto the carpet.

Standing a restrained distance behind me, she says, "We'll live like this forever. Okay? All right? Is that what you want; live here in the gutter and watch, watch, always watching."

"Stop it."

"No, let's send the kids out to play in the lovely street. It's beautiful. Sure. Why not? We should be lucky, right? Isn't that what you always say; lucky just to be alive, to have a roof over our heads. Right. See how many more obscenities Mikey can learn from the scum out there."

Look, I want to say, you don't understand. That's not it. Step closer. The unbearable pageantry of ransacked, gutted beauty is what you're missing. It is truly touching, both powerful and painful, and therefore much more cherished than simple, unscarred beauty.

I continue scanning the houses. My eyes must keep moving. They want to see beyond the street, but vision fades toward the end of the block. I return my gaze to the upper window of the black house.

"What the hell are you watching?"

"Life."

"Rrrr," Her voice shivers. "J e s u s C h r i s t ! ! !" Pam turns and stomps up the stairs. She tries to slam the bedroom door, but the door is lightweight, hollow, and makes little sound, like a fan.

In the window of the black house, a woman with straight, oily hair is sitting, staring down the road with a look of grave longing in her eyes. Her neck is stiff as if she is posing. A stricken mercy beautifies her. Her thick and wrinkled blouse is unbuttoned to the waist. One full breast smoothly extends from the material. The breast is laden and in need of prodding. Upon the nipple, a dark-haired baby sups with determination. The woman cradles the baby in a loose manner. Holding the infant low, her right arm seems weakened by the weight.

Beside her, an unshaven man in a flannel shirt and work trousers pulls up a chair. Leaning down, he gently kisses the top of her head. She does not shift her eyes to acknowledge him. She will not turn her expressionless face.

The man lifts one foot onto the chair, then he shifts his weight and rises, stepping up with the second foot. Standing elevated and perfectly still for a moment, he stares off into the shadowed rear of the room. A tear trail sheens along his cheek. Continual tears descend from the one eye I can see. He is in profile, so I assume symmetry. I assume he is crying from both of his eyes as most of us do. I assume he envisions misery with the soulful perception of two God-given eyes.

Dust has faded his work pants and the hasp sticks as he struggles to unfasten it. It pops loose and the man slips the zipper with ease.

As if on cue, the woman opens her mouth. The man guides himself forward. The woman accepts what he offers. She shapes her lips for enclosure, encouraging what manhood remains.

The man rocks with his knees, slightly backward and forward. He touches the woman's hair. His lips are babbling. I imagine he utters words such as: "Sorry ... sorry (gasping) ... It's the only ... (sniffling toward a sob) ... You know ... I love ... adore you. Please (chest throbbing) Sweet Jesus!"

The woman tightly (perhaps too tightly) clutches the baby while the baby feasts; savouring the milk of delicious misery. The woman – by accepting the man's offering – cradles his need to provide for her. She satisfies the infant as well, by nursing or by strangulation. But she does not look at either of them, as if she is alone.

At my back and upstairs, Pam moves on the other side of the bedroom door, spewing muffled, abrupt words. She is talking to herself. The children are at school. She says something concerning this. Shouting, "Lucky for you. I'd take them and leave."

I stare at the next window. A young girl is sipping wine from a long, delicate glass. She is sitting – with knees bent – on the wide sill behind her window. A black skirt runs down to her ankles. A white tank top presses close to her. The wine is red and the girl's features round out, as if she will laugh. A novel is propped against the slant of her breasts. Occasionally, she peers away from the words and up at the grey sky. She smiles sadly, as if what she has just read was once real. Fanning herself with the book, she tips her head forward to stare down at the street, then – upon seeing nothing – returns to the words. She reads and swallows the wine quickly – as if the novel is guiding her – then pours another glass.

Below the girl, behind a lower window, an obese man is sleeping on a foldaway couch. His blue t-shirt has crept up to expose a pale, cool belly. An old woman stands beside him, staring down. She holds a hand to her mouth and does not say a word. A profound sense of resignation leaves her heavy-headed and thoughtless. A television plays behind her.

"LUCKY," screams Pam. "LUCKY. LUCKY. LUCKY. LUCKY ..."

I step out of my doorway, step down the three gouged concrete steps. My feet are uncovered and there are broken beer bottles strewn along the asphalt fronting of my house. I walk around them. I try – as I must always do – to avoid the absolute cutting power of this street; the complete and dangerous edge that will slice you in two if you resign your strength, if you abandon the mechanisms that force you to believe this is the one and only life. We believe and thus the violence is muted to a place within us where it becomes personal and less disturbing.

Two cars screech past me, flowering a haze of faint, blue smoke. The smell of scorched rubber is harsh in the air. Truant children stand on the chipped curb crooning over the speed. The children's eyes tauntingly stare at me in my bare feet and bare chest. A few bold children point at my naked mid-section and laugh at the stiffness that bobs as if in surrender.

I falter into the center of the street. I see the cars coming. They race side by side. One is dark green, the other white and rusted. They are both heavy cars; sleek and powerful fists that will pull back and punch a hole in this world.

The cars stop, reverse, and then shift down. Suddenly, they are coming fast.

Screeching.

My thoughts unroll like the black scars laid down by those tires, kicking up smoke. I sense the dirt and tiny pebbles pushing against my soles and between my toes.

Raising both hands, I shout, "STOP IT. STOP IT. JUST FUCKING STOP IT."

Steel and chrome race without mercy.

The children are breathless, watching, and rise up on tiptoes.

The young woman lays down her novel to face this lesser vision.

Sensing his climax, the unshaven man cannot control his feeble mouth, dangling open, vacuously agape.

The woman kisses her still baby. Perhaps the infant is sleeping. Perhaps it is dead. The woman has squeezed the life from it or she has cradled it with a firm love that is not death at all.

Springs creak on the pull-out couch as the fat man suddenly awakens; strangely, horribly startled back into his body.

The old woman turns and stares at the television with the false yet exteme sense of belief that weakens this world.

Images on the screen – as on every channel – deceivingly generate expectations for perfection – nothing more, nothing less. The old woman has lost her life to these beauty queen ideals. Now, she steps forward and turns the dial. A preacher's image flickers, his trembling, gifted voice commanding legions.

No one screams a warning (Remember – misery loves company) as the two giant fists punch their hole. And I die. How many times do I die? Lift me from the ground, so we can count them.

Other fine books from The Mercury Press

Order in the Universe and Other Stories by Veronica Ross
Hard Times: A New Fiction Anthology (di Michele, Jones,
    Ducornet, Diamond, McCaffery, et al.)
VIVID: Stories by Five Women (Cadsby, Carey, Howarth,
    Malyon, Wilson)
SKY – A Poem in Four Pieces by Libby Scheier
Transient Light by Steven Smith
Love and Hunger: An Anthology of New Fiction,
    Beverley Daurio, Editor (Atwood, McFadden,
    Jirgens, Truhlar, et al.)
With WK in the Workshop: A Memoir of William Kurelek
    by Brian Dedora
Poetry Markets for Canadians, James Deahl, Editor (with
    the League of Canadian Poets)
The Blue House by Lesley McAllister
Figures in Paper Time by Richard Truhlar
*Ink & Strawberries: An Anthology of Quebec Women's
    Fiction* (Blais, Brossard, Théoret, et al.)
1988: Selected Poems & Texts, 1973-88 by Gerry Shikatani

Please write for our complete catalogue:

THE MERCURY PRESS
(an imprint of Aya Press)
Box 446
Stratford, Ontario
Canada N5A 6T3